Ian Preston grew up surrour
a pretty little village deep in
side. Every night Ian looked f
him a story at bedtime and h
of books and storytelling. Their favourite story was
The Wind in The Willows and it wasn't long before Ian
was writing stories himself.

As a grown-up Ian reads bedtime stories to his own
children and was delighted one day when his daughter
told him all about her imaginary friend, Relly. Ian began
to wonder: where did Relly go and what did he do
when no-one was playing with him?

From that idea he created the world of Imago and
started to write about the adventures of Relly and his
friend Ogi Ogi.

BOOKS IN THE IMAGO SERIES

RELLY, OGI OGI
AND THE
SECRET OF DRAGON'S
TEETH CAVE

Ian Preston

SilverWood

Published in 2020 by SilverWood Books

SilverWood Books Ltd
14 Small Street, Bristol, BS1 1DE, United Kingdom
www.silverwoodbooks.co.uk

ISBN 978-1-78132-924-5 (paperback)
ISBN 978-1-78132-925-2 (ebook)

British Library Cataloguing in Publication Data
A CIP catalogue record for this book is
available from the British Library

Page design and typesetting by SilverWood Books

For dad who always read to me,
no matter how tired he was

CONTENTS

PROLOGUE

BEYOND YOUR IMAGINATION

This tale takes place in a world that's beyond the edge of our imagination. It is the world where our imaginary friends live when you are not playing with them. This world is called Imago.

Imaginary friends come in all shapes, colours and sizes. They take on the appearance that we give them when we are playing with them. If you always wanted a dog when you were little but weren't allowed to have one, you might have imagined that you had one to play with. Maybe it was a scruffy dog who talked and walked on his back legs and played games with you. Now that you are older you might think you are too old to play with your imaginary friend and forgotten all about him. But he hasn't forgotten about you. He's still living happily in Imago with all the other imaginary friends, waiting in case one day you need to talk to him again. That's the things about imaginary friends: they never go away and are always there for you.

Imago is a magnificent place with Imaginos of all descriptions, from talking cupcakes to robots with orange lights for eyes and wheels for legs. Our imaginary friends can change their appearance whenever we play with them. When they return to Imago they stay looking just like they did the last time you thought of them. As we get older and become more concerned with the real world's worries and woes, we think about our imaginary friends less and less until one day we stop thinking about them at all. This is when *The Changing* happens. The Changing is the most important and saddest moment in any Imagino's life. It's the passage from childhood to adulthood for them and from that moment on their appearance and character is fixed exactly as it was the very last time their child thought of them. You see, when we stop thinking about them and playing with them they don't die; no, they stay living in their world, always hoping that one day we might imagine and play with them again.

CHAPTER ONE

THE COUNCIL CHAMBER

The Council of Imago was sitting around a large wooden table in the Great Hall of the castle. The Council was made up of six Imaginos and together they ruled the world of Imago. There was Marjorie, Ma Westwood, Claus, Mithren, Lionbear and Goggles and they were quite an odd-looking bunch. Ma Westwood looked like a giant goose; Marjorie, a girl; Lionbear, a cross between a lion and a bear; Claus, a boy with clogs and a pointy hat; Goggles, a squiggly mess with a huge pair of glasses; and Mithren looked like a tall elf with long blonde hair. If you were to peer in through a window of the Great Hall, and you didn't know about Imago, you'd wonder where on Earth you were.

The Council's six members were huddled closely together around one end of an enormous oak table, studying a large map of the whole of Imago. Imago is a huge world which stretches from the Endless Ocean in the North to the rich, green, Southern lands. The Endless Ocean is a beautiful, deep-blue that glitters prettily in the sun. If you climb to the highest peak of the Northern Mountains you get the most fabulous view of Imago. As the sun rises in the East, the deep blue of the ocean sits next to the bright oranges of the Eastern desert plains.

Looking back to the South and West, you can see many towns, villages and even the castle where the Council sits, or stands as they were on this particular evening. The woodlands to the South stretch on as far as the eye can see.

The Council of Imago was meeting to discuss the General. He's a wicked Imagino who'd recently tried to take over the world of Imago but worryingly, had been missing for over a month. He'd fled the castle when his spell over Marjorie had been broken and no-one knew where he was. The Imaginos didn't know how but somehow the General had put Marjorie into a trance. Whilst under his spell she'd declared herself Princess of the land and begun a rule of tyranny and misery. And the wicked General had supported and encouraged her. He had stood at her side and helped her to make decisions about who to arrest and who to banish from the world, which could be anyone who upset the General in the slightest way. Princess Marjorie had locked up all the imaginary friends she thought were ugly as well as anyone who'd disagreed with her. She even threw Imaginos in prison if she thought they'd just looked at her a bit funny. Under her rule, the Council of Imago had been disbanded and imprisoned and the General had taken control of the guards. There was no-one left who could stop her getting her own way in everything.

But with the help of two imaginative girls called Abby and Jane and their imaginary friends Relly and Ogi Ogi, Marjorie had realised she had been put under a spell by the General, who was using her to take control of the land. The friends had helped save Marjorie and break the spell and ever since, Marjorie had done everything she could to make up for the horrible things she had done. She'd proved herself to be a quick-witted, thoughtful and kind Imagino. When the new Council had been formed, Ma Westwood, the castle's friendly cook, had suggested that Marjorie join too and help them find the General. So far not a trace of them had been found. The most recent sighting had been from a villager in the North, who thought she had seen a band of Imaginos heading towards the Eastern desert plains.

The Council had placed counters that looked like little flags stuck in corks on the map to show the areas they'd searched. Ma Westwood was confused. She sat deep in thought, rubbing her beak with the tip of her wing.

'We've searched high and low for the General. He's either disappeared or he's being hidden by some traitors,' she said.

'Well, they might be under his spell,' Marjorie replied. 'They may not even know what they're doing. I didn't know what I was doing until Relly and Ogi Ogi travelled to the mountains and broke the spell I was under. We've sent messages to The Prospector who lives in the mountains to see if he's seen the General, but he has not replied.'

The Prospector was a loud Imagino who lived deep under the mountains searching for gold and gems. He'd helped Relly and Ogi Ogi on their last adventure by letting them use a magic stone he had found under the mountain. They'd used the stone to break the General's spell and free Imago from his rule of tyranny.

'If the General is heading north then it can't be good news,' said Ma Westwood. 'He might have found out about The Prospector's magic stone or he could be trying to steal gems to buy himself an army. We must try and stop him.'

'We should get a message to The Prospector as soon as we can,' said Mithren.

'I'd love to go,' said Lionbear. 'Why, I wouldn't mind climbing those mountains and looking across our beautiful world.'

'Well it's a long way you need to set of straight away,' said Marjorie.

Lionbear was Captain of Imago's guards, he'd been promoted after the General disappeared. He liked the job because he got to wear an extra red feather in his cap. He quickly blew the little trumpet they used to call the soldiers into the castle's Great Hall. The room echoed with footsteps as dozens of Imaginos came running into hall.

'Right you lovely lot,' cried Lionbear, 'who would like to accompany me on an adventure to capture that stinking General?'

Whilst most Imaginos love an adventure, the General had been a horrid master when he'd been giving the orders. He'd even thrown some of them up in the dungeon for failing to carry out his orders. Bizzwhinny, a small Imagino that looked like a big mouse, had refused to push someone into a muddy stream and found himself locked up.

'I don't want to end up in the dungeons again,' said Bizzwhinny.

'Don't be scared of that gas bag!' cried Lionbear. 'He's going to get his comeuppance when we finally catch up with him. Come on, who's with me!'

The crowd of Imaginos cheered and Lionbear led them to the armoury to gather up their swords. They were soon marching up the road to the North singing a happy song as they clomped along:

Off to the Northern Mountains we stomp
Hear our feet go clomp clomp clomp!
We will catch that stinking rotter
To stop that evil smelly plotter!

It was one of those cold, crisp Autumn days when the blue sky was beautifully decorated with the reds, greens and yellows of the leaves on the trees. Relly and Ogi Ogi were sitting on the bridge listening to their old friend Glump. Relly looked like a tall boy with brownish skin, purple hair and red eyes. Ogi Ogi was shorter and he had no real body to speak of, although his arms and legs were solid enough. He was slightly transparent with a dark green tinge and a habit of letting off the most fruit-some bottom burps, especially and somewhat suspiciously, it seemed, when Jane's daddy was in the room. Relly's child is called Abby and Ogi Ogi's child is called Jane and as so often happens in Imago, the two children are best friends, just like their imaginary friends. Relly and Ogi Ogi are both a little bit mischievous, which is really a polite way of saying naughty. But Abby and Jane love playing with their lively creations.

The bridge on which they were sitting wasn't just any old bridge, it was 'The Bridge'. It was the very bridge that Glump had chosen to live under. After all, where else would a troll live other than under a bridge?

Glump was very old and extremely ugly. He was a huge Imagino with legs like tree trunks and hands the size of buckets. He had a wart on the end of his nose the size of a chicken's egg and his teeth looked like a piano's keys after the piano had fallen out of a window. Some of them looked like they were sticking out sideways and there were big gaps where teeth were missing. His straggly hair had mostly fallen out while he had been in the dungeons so now the top of his head was like a shiny green bowling ball with just a few tufts of hair sticking out of the top. But Glump was only ugly on the outside because on the inside he was beautiful. He was one of the kindest and funniest Imaginos you could meet. His stories, laughter and songs would make you chuckle so much that after a few minutes of listening to him you would forget the warts on the end of his nose, his straggly hair and missing teeth, and you would see the person he really was on the inside.

Glump wasn't bothered by his looks. He'd already undergone the Changing and spent many years getting used to the fact he was a troll, warts and all. But Relly and Ogi Ogi hadn't yet undergone the Changing, which meant the next time Abby and Jane played with them, they might change their appearance. If Jane decided that Ogi Ogi was pink when she played with him, then when he came back to Imago he'd be pink. After this, if Jane never thought about Ogi Ogi again he'd stay pink forever. He would still get older though, which is why Glump looks so very old. His child was now a very old man.

Glump, Ogi Ogi and Relly sat on the edge of the bridge swinging their legs, but Glump couldn't really swing his legs as his feet were stuck firmly in the gloopy mud. They'd been playing in this very spot when the guards had arrested him at the beginning of their last adventure.

'Well, you two,' Glump said, after a while, 'my bones

ache today more than they did yesterday and more than last year. I don't usually moan but the coming of winter makes me feel like I'm turning into stone. Sometimes in stories trolls turn into stone, you know. I hope I don't get so cold that I finally turn into a huge block of granite. I dare say someone could chip my nose off and use it as a door stop.' As he chuckled he sounded like a cross between a cement mixer full of broken bricks and the funniest belly laugh you'd ever heard.

'I've had a fine life living under this bridge with the water running past. I've always loved the sound of the stream. Throughout the year it's been a comfort to hear it tinkle and trickle by. In the spring at night you can hear the frogs croaking and at this time of year, I can watch all manner of things floating past, like leaves, twigs and branches. It's cold in winter, especially when it snows,' he said. 'But I don't think I could live anywhere else. It's been the best home I could ever have hoped for.'

'Maybe you could build a little house next to the bridge,' suggested Ogi Ogi. 'We'd help you, if you wanted that is.'

'Oh no, I couldn't possibly,' Glump replied. 'It's a very kind offer and I thank you very much. But a troll is meant to be living under a bridge and that's just what feels right to me. Do you know, a goat even crossed over my bridge once?'

'A goat?' said Relly.

'That's right, it made my day,' said Glump. 'I couldn't believe it when an Imagino that looked just like a goat came trotting by. You see goats and trolls have a long history. In fact, did I ever tell you why Peter thought of me and how I ended up as a troll?' Glump said.

'No I don't think so,' Relly replied, excitedly.

Glump stretched out and got ready to tell them both

a story. He cleared his throat and it sounded like someone banging a bag of pebbles on a wall. Relly and Ogi Ogi shuffled closer because they knew it was going to be one of his super stories. Once they were comfortable he began to tell them the story of Peter and the goat.

'Peter grew up on a farm. It was a dairy farm so they mostly had black and white cows called friesians. But his mum was an animal lover, so many of the smaller fields were crammed full of all sorts of different creatures. He felt very lucky to have so many animals and his friends loved coming to visit the cows, chickens, ducks, sheep, cats, goats, geese and of course the little dog Pip.

Peter caught the bus to school, like many others who lived in the countryside. The path to the road and the bus stop ran through the field of goats. One of the goats, the biggest male goat who was the leader of the tribe, was particularly fearsome. He spent his days strutting around the field like a peacock. The minute that Peter entered the field, the big goat would stop eating and begin staring at him. Peter would begin walking across the field slowly and the goat would normally just stare at him. But sometimes the goat would charge at him and he would need to run to the bus stop. It was normally a pretty short distance, so Peter had time to get there before the big goat could catch him. He'd jumped over the stile at the end of the field many times, with the goat bearing down on him.

His school chums would peer out of the windows of the waiting bus. If the goat had started to chase him they would be cheering for Peter to escape. By the time Peter made it to the bus, the driver would be yelling at the children to sit down. Peter would dash on to the bus with a red face and they would all shout, 'Bravo!'

Now, as you know, a troll is the sworn enemy of a goat. Peter had read the story about the Three Billy Goats Gruff so he knew this. One of Peter's earliest memories featured the big goat. He had been in the farm's garden playing in a paddling pool on a hot summer's day. He must have been about three years old at the time. He could remember throwing a beach ball to his mum, who'd caught it and thrown it back. Suddenly the peaceful splashing in the pool had been shattered by a crash at the garden gate followed by a terrifying sound of splintering wood. The big goat had broken free from the field and was smashing his way through the garden gate! Peter's mum had scooped Peter up in her arms and run back towards the house just in the nick of time. After several ferocious head butts, the goat had charged into the garden and launched itself at the beach ball. He skewered the ball with his horns and then began bucking around the garden trying to shake it off.

It was shortly after this event that Peter's mum had read him the story of the Three Billy Goats Gruff, which may not have been a very good idea given how scared Peter now was of goats. But he was a brave boy and decided then that the farm needed a troll, who would be the sworn enemy of the big goat, and keep him and his mother safe. It was about then that I appeared and became Peter's fearless friend in the ongoing battle with that goat and any other manner of adventures he might create.'

'Blimey,' said Ogi Ogi, 'that goat sounds completely bonkers. Why didn't the farmer sell him if he was so angry and violent?'

'Well he needed the big goat to keep all the other goats in the tribe in line. Goats can be a very rowdy and ill-disciplined rabble. On top of that the big goat became a bit of a local celebrity. A group of criminals had begun stealing farm vehicles like tractors and combine harvesters. One night they came to Peter's farm in the dead of night and parked their getaway car in the bus stop. The burglars must have started creeping across the field as quietly as possible. Little did they know that an angry goat lay in wait.'

'A guard goat, whatever next!' declared Relly.

Glump laughed deeply, 'The goat must have seen them crossing the field and then charged at them. The burglars hadn't been expecting a high-speed goat, so the first they knew about it was when one of his sharp horns stabbed into a burglar's bottom. He howled with pain, which alerted the second burglar. He turned and fled for the getaway car, but before he could get there the goat caught up and butted him into the hedge. The scuffle made a tremendous noise and the whole farm was soon awake. Peter's dad dashed out with his shotgun and held the burglars whilst they waited for the police. The story of the Guard Goat was reported in the national papers and everything. The headline read, '*Goat catches the Tattlesfield Tractor Thief*' and people came from all over the country to take pictures of him.'

'Maybe the goat was shy and didn't like being a celebrity,' said Ogi Ogi.

They all looked at each other and started laughing again. The water steadily trickled by and the day with it. A patch of golden leaves floated past and this made Relly think of the mines in the Northern Mountains. He rubbed his chin thoughtfully. 'I wonder how The Prospector and Small Bear are. Small Bear really wanted to explore the mines and find some treasure. I wonder if he's managed to find a huge pile of mountain of gold yet.'

The Prospector and Small Bear had once helped the two friends reach the top of the Northern Mountains. They needed to reach the top to use a magic stone to enter the dreams of their children. Both The Prospector and small Bear had stayed behind when the Eagle had flown Relly and Ogi Ogi back to Creatown.

'I expect Small Bear has gone deep into the mines to find caverns with walls that sparkle with diamonds, rubies and sapphires,' said Ogi Ogi.

'I should imagine there is a room piled high with nuggets of gold as big as your fist,' Relly replied, excitedly.

Glump smiled, 'I'm not sure you'd know what to do with a pile of gold and I doubt it would buy you any more happiness than you can find for yourselves.' But the two young friends weren't listening to his wisdom. They were lost in a wondrous world of mine shafts and caverns filled with riches.

'I bet we could take a ride in one of the mine carts,' said Ogi Ogi. 'We could zoom through the tunnels with the lights of the cavern whizzing by.'

'What a great idea!' Relly said. 'Why don't we go and see them. I bet they'd like to know what's been happening here and we could see the Eagle and his egg at the same time. Would you like to come with us, Glump? You'd love The Prospector, he's full of interesting stories as well. I bet you'd get on famously.'

'Thank you, but no,' said Glump. 'I need to start collecting leaves and branches to build a bit of a shelter around the base of the bridge. It takes longer and longer each year, but without it the wind whistles through here like a tornado. The colder I get, the more my knees crack in the morning: sometimes they sound like a giant cracking two boulders together. What's more, my legs would be worn down to stumps if I tried to walk as far as the mountains. No, I will wait here and watch the world go by until you return and I will look forward to you telling me all about it.'

'Well don't go off and get yourself arrested again,' Relly joked.

'I don't know, those dungeons weren't so bad. The damp made my bones ache something rotten, but there were plenty of people to speak to. Why, I made a few friends down in the dungeons. I met this funny frog called Kummit. He had loads of warts like me. He lives in a swamp to the South West where this stream meets the southern woods. He was full of stories about the Imaginos who live there. There's a crocodile that plays a banjo. Fancy that, eh?' said Glump.

'We saw Marjorie sentencing him when she was still under that evil General's spell. He begged them not to take him to the dungeons where there wouldn't be any water. They had to drag the poor thing away,' Relly replied.

'Well we both missed the water, but we talked about the stream and the swamp often and that kept our spirits up. One corner of the prison cell was really damp and sometimes there would be enough water to splash our feet in. We even had a sing-song one evening, but the guards didn't like that. They came storming down to the cells and started bellowing at us. One of them had a funny face with a big red nose,' Glump said.

'That would be the Captain of the Guards,' Ogi Ogi said. 'I bet he's enjoying that puddle now.' They all laughed at the thought of him mopping up in the cells.

CHAPTER THREE

FESTIVE FUN WAITING FOR CHRISTMAS

Christmas was coming and as any child will tell you, or adult if they let themselves, this is the best time of year. Abby was at Jane's house where they were watching TV together and enjoying the last day of the half term holiday. That meant that they only had a few more weeks of school and then it would be Christmas. No more school, instead they would be at home with their families watching films, eating chocolates and unwrapping presents.

The two girls were the best of friends and whilst they had some differences, they both loved making up stories and games, and more importantly for this story, playing with their imaginary friends. Jane, Ogi Ogi's child, was taller than Abby. Jane had brown hair in tight curls, and when she smiled deep dimples appeared on her cheeks. Unlike Abby, Jane could be a bit shy when meeting new people for the first time. She loved playing sports and climbing trees.

Abby had chestnut red hair and a smattering of pretty freckles on her nose, which she scrunched up when she smiled. She was a bit louder than Jane, and normally the one who got caught when they were getting into mischief. Abby loved books but when she wasn't reading she could be found designing dresses or outfits, often trying to use her little brother Jack as a model.

The two girls often enjoyed play dates at each other's houses. Abby loved visiting Jane's house for two main reasons: her little brother Jack wasn't around to suddenly burst into the room and knock everything over; and, Jane's older sister Isadora was there. Isadora was three years older than the girls and Abby thought that she was the coolest girl she'd ever met. Jane disagreed because she could run faster than Isadora and to her, that was all that mattered. Isadora had her own YouTube fashion channel and was allowed to wear make up at the weekends, which she would apply at her dressing table, whilst gazing intently into her enormous mirror surrounded by colour-changing lights. Abby would have loved to have had such a fancy dressing table which was covered in an array of fabulously interesting looking make up cases, pots and bottles, Abby often tried to find a reason to go into Isadora's room and ask her a question but most of the time she'd push the door shut and tell them to, 'Run off and play with your invisible friends!'

If Isadora only knew, thought Abby, in fact she could hardly believe it herself. It had been earlier that year whilst she'd been having a perfectly wonderful dream about fairies, that suddenly Relly had appeared. That moment had changed everything. What was perhaps, even more surprising to Abby than discovering her invisible friend is actually real, was that on the very same night, Jane's imaginary friend had also appeared. Isadora might think that their imaginary friends are just the invisible fantasies of her baby sister and her baby sister's friend, but to the girls, they are as real as you and me.

The two girls finished watching TV and dashed up the stairs together laughing. As they reached the top, Isadora's door slammed shut. 'I'm recording a video in a minute so keep the noise down in La La Land, please.'

The girls looked at each other and burst into more peals of laughter. They raced into Jane's room where they jumped onto her bed and settled down to begin thinking about the last few weeks of term at school. They both loved the end of winter term and all he preparations for Christmas but best of all was the Nativity Performance. They enjoyed taking part in the Nativity immensely, despite both being cast as sheep last year. They started to chatter excitedly about this year's performance and wondered what parts they might be.

'I hope I'm Mary or the Angel Gabriel,' Jane said.

'I bet it will be Joanne Reid again,' Abby replied. 'Last year she was Mary and the year before she was the star who narrated the whole story. She always gets the best parts. It's not fair.'

'Well I'm not sure I'd like to learn all those lines,' said Jane, 'and you don't get to do any song or dance routines if you get the main parts. You just get to read out lines and you need to act sensibly. I thought the Christmas puddings *Dance Of The Desserts* was the best bit of last year's show. I'd much rather be a fluffy sheep than Mary. Mary has to sit at the front with a tea towel on her head wearing one of her mum's old dresses.' The two girls looked at each other and then burst into laughter again.

'I've got a good idea,' Jane said. 'Why don't we put our own Nativity?'

'That's a great idea,' Abby replied. 'We could be whoever we want and we could get Relly and Ogi Ogi to help us. Before we start we'd better plan out the characters and the plot.'

'We know the plot,' said Jane.

'I know that,' said Abby, 'but the school always add

some extra bits, like Father Christmas or even parts of the Christmas lunch!'

'Well I'm not going to be a turkey or a sprout,' laughed Jane.

The two girls started collecting up all of Jane's teddies. 'We can have the three bears instead of the three kings and your doll Magdalen can be Mary,' Abby said.

Soon the bedroom had been rearranged into a scene in Bethlehem with Jane's battered dolls' house as the stable, a rough cardboard box as a cradle and a Tiny Tears baby doll as Jesus.

'Why don't we film it?' suggested Abby.

'Great idea!' said Jane. 'We can ask Isadora for her mobile phone.'

Jane ran to Isadora's room and was about to knock at the door when it was flung open. A partly made-up Isadora answered the door, fuming. Half her hair was held up haphazardly with a big clip and the other side of her hair had been divided into sections and wound around little sponge sausages to make it curly. She had painted her lips with bright red lipstick and coloured her eyelids with a bright green eye shadow. In one hand she held a sharp eye liner pencil and in the other, a hair drier, which she now waved rather menacingly at the girls. She was also frowning, which made her half made-up face look even more ridiculous. She looked like a crazy clown who'd fallen into a make-up box.

'You two squealing is sooooo distracting. You have no idea! I'm in the middle of a very delicate hair operation and I need silence,' snapped Isadora.

Jane looked up and smiled. She knew if she laughed Isadora would probably explode with rage, and it looked like an explosion had happened in her bedroom already. Abby came dashing along the landing and skidded into the back of Jane, almost knocking her to the floor. The two girls steadied themselves and stood, smiling up at Isadora. Isadora harumphed loudly and slammed the door. The two girls looked at each other and then ran back to their room. Once inside they began rolling around the floor laughing.

'Why don't we borrow your mum's phone?' suggested Abby.

'She's got an old camera we can use,' said Jane. 'Once we've finished, we could upload it to YouTube and start our own TV channel.'

After another half an hour or so they'd borrowed a camera from Jane's mum, found some fresh batteries and set it up so they could film their Nativity. 'I think Relly should record the sound,' suggested Abby.

'Ogi Ogi could be the director and look after the camera,' Jane said.

'Well not if he makes lots of parping noises,' laughed Abby.

Back in Imago, Ogi Ogi and Relly were just arriving back at their house to start packing for their journey when the two friends felt that sinking feeling in their stomach again. They looked at each other and smiled because they were crossing over together, which meant the girls were almost definitely playing together, so all four of them were going to have fun. They began to feel as if they were falling. Relly imagined himself going round and round like water into a huge plug hole. The plug hole was probably like a well in time and space. Once they'd gone into it, he imagined himself going down a huge tunnel-like slide that came out in the girls' world, Earth.

Relly and Ogi Ogi landed in Jane's bedroom and looked at each other. It looked like they might be taking part in a Nativity. The two girls had decided to be the angels and would, therefore, narrate the story. Relly and Ogi Ogi were delighted to discover their roles as camera and sound men. Rather than temporarily turn into shepherds, sheep or even worse a donkey, they had a major role in the creative process.

'We need someone to say *action*,' said Jane.

'Oh Ogi Ogi had better do that,' Abby replied. 'He will need one of those special movie clip boards and a special director's hat. Like a French one, you know, a beret.'

'He will look absolutely splendiferous with a marvellous beret,' Jane said. 'I think it should be a blue one with a red feather for effect.'

Ogi Ogi and Relly looked at the makeshift Nativity scene. The stable (dolls' house) was now crammed full of teddies, dolls and plastic animals. The two girls had transformed themselves into angels with a couple of old cream dresses, some fairy wings, an old frisbee as a halo and a large quantity of gold glitter in their hair. The glitter had spread itself around the room, as glitter tends to, making the whole scene sparkle rather magically.

'ACTION!' the girls cried together and the Nativity began.

Now I'm sure you know most of the nativity story but it's worth hearing the best bits to get a feel for the show. The three kings, played by the dwarfs Happy, Bashful and Sleepy, delivered a set of unusual gifts to the giant baby Jesus Tiny Tears who filled almost the entire ground floor of the dolls' house. The girls decided to improve the traditional gifts of gold, frankincense and myrrh because neither of them knew what frankincense or myrrh were, or what you do with them, and they didn't have anything gold.

'If you'd just had a baby I think you'd probably be hungry,' said Jane.

'Oh definitively,' Abby said. 'I think Mary would need some chocolate to give her some energy, don't you?'

'I'd think she'd need a bar of chocolate or two at the least. It's a good job we brought some upstairs with us because the film crew will need feeding as well. Plus all of this narrating is pretty tiring, so we will need some too,' Jane said, nodding knowledgably.

Jane broke off two pieces of chocolate from one of the bars, which she placed next to the crib. She shared the remaining chocolate between herself, Abby and much to their delight, the two imaginary friends. (I'm sure you're thinking, hang-on...how can an imaginary friend eat something solid? Well if the girls imagine their friends eating the chocolate, then of course they will taste the chocolate. In fact they will feel all the same wondrous tastes that we do. Ogi Ogi even briefly turned brown as the chocolate slowly dissolved into his body.)

'So, we don't need frankincense now,' Abby said, 'but I'm not sure that Mary and Joseph would want Myrrh either. It's meant to smell nice and I think you can use it as a medicine, but wouldn't they want some nice clean towels and a bar of soap?'

'That's a good idea,' said Jane. 'Mary can wash the baby then so he's nice and clean for all his visitors.' Jane dashed off into the bathroom and came back with a face cloth and a brand new bar of soap. 'There,' she said, 'now they will all smell lovely.'

'What about the gold?' Abby asked.

'Good point,' said Jane. 'Gold was probably quite useful, but I don't have any.' Jane thought about this problem for a minute or two before she had an idea. 'I do have a two pound coin though in my money tin. Back in the time of King Herod, a two pound coin was probably worth a lot of money. So hopefully that will be enough to help them out.'

After the three dwarfs had provided Mary (one of Jane's better clothed Barbies) and Joseph (a meerkat teddy bear) with the gifts, the two angels recounted the Nativity story whilst Ogi Ogi and Relly recorded the entire show. Relly particularly enjoyed pretending to move the microphone around the room to make sure that they had good sound quality and Ogi Ogi spent most of the time pretending to sit in a director's chair. There he sat, waving his arms around wildly and at one point he leapt up and began pointing at those Nativity animals that were making too much noise.

Once Mary, Joseph and Jesus (Barbie, Meercat and Tiny Tears) had fled King Herod's guards, Ogi Ogi cried 'Cut, that's a wrap!' None of them was really sure what this meant, but they were pretty sure that you said it at the end of filming. The two girls immediately crowded around the camera and began watching the film. They both laughed from the depths of their bellies as they watched the story. Listening to your voice on film or in a recording is always funny for some reason. As the two girls began to talk about posting the film on YouTube, the two Imaginos could feel the tug of Imago.

Relly faded first and began to tumble back through the divide to Imago with Ogi Ogi following not far behind. As the two friends landed in Imago not far from their home, Relly looked up at Ogi Ogi and burst into laughter.

'What's so funny?' Ogi Ogi asked.

'Your hat,' Relly replied trying not to laugh again.

Ogi Ogi felt the top of his head and found the beret sitting there. 'Oh no!' he said, 'I don't want to be stuck with this silly hat for the rest of my life. It's blue and it's got a stupid feather sticking out of it. I look like I have a peacock nesting on my head.'

It was quite possible that Ogi Ogi would always have the beret unless Jane imagined him without it and if she grew up and stopped playing with him he'd be stuck with it for the rest of his life. Of course, he could take it off and throw it away but every morning when he woke up there it would be, having appeared mysteriously on his head and he'd have to throw it away again.

'Come on,' said Relly, 'we've got an adventure to have, so stop worrying about a silly hat. The girls were just using it for filming the Nativity, I'm sure it'll be gone next time you see Jane.'

CHAPTER FOUR

JOURNEY TO CREATOWN

Whenever Relly and Ogi Ogi went home they liked to play '*Who Can Spy The Chimney Pot?*' They'd built the house together out of bits and bobs they'd come across like old washing machines, table tops, drain pipes, a water wheel and lots of cardboard boxes filled with straw. The chimney took the smoke from the wood burner and piped it away. The first chimney had been too short and smoke had billowed into the house, so they'd built a higher one to keep their home clear. On the second attempt, Ogi Ogi had been determined to keep the house smoke free, so he ended up building the tallest chimney in Imago (well on a little house anyway). The house itself was about three metres high, but if you added the chimney it was almost ten. On the top of the chimney, they'd added a weather vane made out of a sign they'd found at Brook Lane Farm saying, '*Warning, sheep crossing.*'

As they walked up the final hill towards their house they each began to move faster. They'd walked this path a thousand times, so they both knew the exact point at which the chimney would appear. Rather than wait until they got there and remember to shout, they would both start speed walking in a very comical way up the hill until one of them cracked and started running. By the time they reached the crest of the hill, they'd both be running flat out. Whoever got to the top first would cry, 'I can see the chimney from here!' and then they'd both collapse on the floor laughing.

Today was no different. Ogi Ogi and Relly were both running as fast as possible by the time they reached the top of the hill. They were side by side as they arrived at the top and they both shouted 'Chimney!' at the same time and then charged down the other side. It was a dead heat. So rather than stop or fall over laughing, they carried on running to see who could get to the door first. The first one there would ring the doorbell. Relly had found on old bell in Creatown last year and used it to make a doorbell. It was like a smaller version of the ones you get in church towers. He'd hung it next to the door and used a piece of red and blue cord for the bell rope. Because the bell was so heavy, you had to pull on it really hard to make it dong. If you ran up to it, swung on the cord and then let go, the bell would dong at least three times.

By the time they reached the house both of them were out of breath. Relly arrived a fraction of a second before Ogi Ogi and jumped on to the rope. He swung mightily and let go, flying off into the flower beds and the bell let out three fabulous dongs. Ogi Ogi doubled up with laughter as Relly sat up, mud falling out of his hair.

'I won, I won,' panted Relly.

The two friends tumbled into their house and began hunting for all the things they might need. It was a long journey to the mountains and the last time they'd set out on an adventure, they'd hardly packed a thing. They'd set off for the castle with no real idea of where they were going or what they might find. Relly set about rummaging through drawers and cupboards for their backpacks and supplies: a shovel, just in case they got stuck in snow; a tent; a rope for climbing; sturdy boots for walking; bandages; matches and tinder for making fire; and the map that Ogi Ogi had drawn once they'd returned home. Ogi Ogi began gathering up the clothes they needed for the trip. It was already late Autumn and Winter was coming so he packed their thick coats and hats.

After half an hour they'd gathered everything they might need and made a batch of sandwiches to keep themselves going.

'We'd better lock our little house up,' said Relly.

'Have you got the map?' asked Ogi Ogi.

'Yes, it's here,' Relly replied.

He took out the map and opened it up. Ogi Ogi had drawn the map over several long summer evenings. The map featured all of the places they'd visited on their last adventure and the things they'd seen from the top of the Northern Mountains.

'Well it's a big old place. We'd better hurry to Creatown if we want to rest there tonight,' Relly said.

'That's a good idea,' Ogi Ogi replied. 'We could see if Father Rhyme has come home yet. He disappeared to avoid being arrested by the General and his guards but it's strange that he's not returned home now that the General has been banished.'

Relly rubbed his chin and looked thoughtfully towards the Northern Mountains. 'Hmmmm,' he replied, 'you're right. I thought he'd come back once the Council of Imago was restored, but no-one has seen or heard of him. It's like he's completely vanished. If he hasn't returned we should see if we can find any clues to his whereabouts.'

The two friends looked at each other excitedly. Searching for clues sounded like detective work and that sounded like an adventure. So now, rather than just visiting friends, they were on a mission. Relly locked the door and placed the key under the fourth stone behind the pond at the bottom of the garden. Ogi Ogi checked to make sure they'd packed a flask of tea and some biscuits. Ogi Ogi liked his tea with four sugars, which Relly said meant he had a 'sweet tooth' but as far as he could tell, his tooth wasn't made of anything sweet. Finally he checked that the doors and windows were locked and the two friends waved good bye to their colourful house and set off for Creatown.

The hill to Glump's bridge was behind them as they headed West towards the town. The path ran alongside large fields and meadows. The grass in the meadows swayed in the wind as the skies began to darken. In the last half an hour it had got colder; the air carrying that slightly damp smell that meant rain was sure to come soon. The wind had begun to blow harder and distant trees were beginning to bend Luckily for the two friends, the wind was behind them and they began to walk faster as the wind had started to blow them along. Every now and again a strong gust would come and they'd skip forward.

'I think it's going to start raining soon,' Relly said nervously.

'We're going to get blown away in a minute,' Ogi Ogi replied. 'If we had a kite, we could probably fly there. If it starts to rain we might have to try and find cover somewhere. How close is Nutty's wood?'

'I'm not sure. It can't be far from here because last time

we went through it, we were on our way from the Castle to Creatown. Do you remember we left the wood and we joined the road to the town?'

'That's right. It can't be far from here,' said Ogi Ogi.

As they finished speaking, lightning flashed then two or three seconds later there was a loud crash of thunder. 'The storm must be close!' cried Relly. 'I think we need to head to the top of the path and then turn left towards those woods. I'm not sure, but I think that's his wood.'

The two friends started to jog up the path with the wind howling behind them. They reached the cross roads at the top of the hill as the heavens opened and the rain came pouring down. It may sound silly, but this was the sort of rain that's really wet. The drops aren't drops at all. It feels like someone's tipping a glass of water on your head and when the rain hits the ground it bounces back up again. To make things worse, it was very cold.

Relly and Ogi Ogi turned to the left and sprinted down the path towards the woods. A small stream had formed next to the path and they created huge splashes of water as they dashed onwards. The wind was now at their side so, rather than blow them along, it was pushing them sideways. The woods were only a hundred metres away when the next bolt of lightning struck. This time it was very close indeed. The noise of the colossal thunder clap left a ringing in their ears. The two friends sprinted into the woods and then looked back at the field. As the ringing started to fade, they could hear another strange noise: 'Cr-cr-cr-cr-cr-crrrraacccccccckkkKK.' They stood under the trees of the wood, staring into the field with their mouths open. The noise sounded as if it was coming from the corner of the field.

'A tree is falling!' screamed Relly. 'The lightning must have hit it!'

'It's smoking!' Ogi Ogi cried.

As they stood watching the tree, it slowly broke in half. It looked like someone was peeling a banana as the tree trunk fell apart. Suddenly the rain started to fall even harder and another huge flash of lightning made them jump. The two friends sprinted deeper into the woods without looking back. The thick canopy of woods protected them from the rain. They could hear the rain above them but inside the wood it was only dripping down occasionally.

'Nutty lived at the centre of the wood somewhere,' Relly said. 'If we keep going in a straight line, we should find him.'

The two friends could just see a glimmer of light ahead which they knew must be Nutty's glade. Full of excitement they waded through the thick ferns that grew under the trees until they reached the edge of the glade where they stopped to let their eyes adjust to the light. The rain was falling heavily in the glade and they couldn't see the squirrel anywhere. Something didn't feel quite right and the two friends slowly crept around the edge towards the hut. It looked deserted.

'Shall we have a look inside?' Relly asked, nervously.

'It doesn't look like anyone's home. I can't imagine the squirrel leaving his wood behind. Something must be wrong; he loves his plants,' Ogi Ogi said.

The two friends slowly approached the hut. They crouched down behind the window and cautiously popped their heads over the window sill. The hut was completely empty. All the furniture had gone and it looked as if no-one had been there for weeks. The rain was still hammering down and the two friends were now soaked to the skin. They looked at each other and nodded. They quickly scampered around to the front of the hut and let themselves in. The hut might be empty, but at least it was dry! They looked at the fire place and luckily there was still a stack of logs next to it. Relly quickly started to build the fire.

The Prospector had taught the two Imaginos to light fires. Ogi Ogi took some dry wool from his pack and poked it in amongst the logs. He took the two pieces of flint and rubbed them together, sending sparks flying into the wool. Carefully he blew on the sparks until the wool began to glow with little orange flames. Soon the dry logs were crackling as the flames danced in front of them. Within ten minutes the two friends were sitting in front of a warm fire with their wet coats and trousers hanging off coat pegs on the back of the hut's door. The centre of the storm had passed over them. The rain was still falling heavily, but the thunder was quieter now as it had moved further away. Outside the large puddle which had formed in the glade was starting to grow into a small pond.

'I wonder if we will see any frogs,' Relly said. 'If it keeps raining like this, we will end up with a lake outside.'

There was a sudden loud scraping noise. *Scrrrrr-crrrrrr-pppp*. 'What was that?' said Relly, startled. *Scrrrrr-crrrrrr-pppp-pppper* came the noise again.

The two Imaginos edged towards the window and slowly peered over the top of the window sill. The sun had begun to fade, leaving a deep purple sky full of mist from the rain. Outside the glade still looked deserted. The noise had stopped and all they could hear was the rain splashing in the growing puddle.

Suddenly, out of nowhere, a flash of blue came flying towards them. Nutty, the blue squirrel, leapt from the top of the nut store. The tip of his tail brushed the top of Relly's head as the squirrel somersaulted over their heads. Ogi Ogi stumbled backwards and fell onto his back with his legs waggling around in the air.

'Woo-ha, a roasted chestnut to warm you,' the squirrel beamed at them.

'You're here!' Relly whooped in delight.

'Where else?' asked the squirrel. 'This is my home, after all.'

'Well it was completely empty,' said Relly.

'Totally deserted,' said Ogi Ogi as he sat up.

Nutty laughed and took the chestnuts out of the fire. 'Well that's a longer tale,' said the squirrel, 'but first let's eat, I'm famished.'

After they'd eaten, the squirrel began to tell them his story. The Council had ordered that the General be arrested. To avoid being caught he and his gang had run away and hidden in the squirrel's wood where they set-up camp in the glade. Poor Nutty had to leave his comfy house and hide in the trees where he could do nothing but watch as they ate his nuts and trampled his beautiful, flower-filled garden. The mean, cruel gang stayed for about a week and several times each day the squirrel watched as the General sneaked off to a hut. Eventually curiosity made the squirrel brave and he followed the General to the hut and waited outside, standing on tiptoes at the window so he could just about see in over the sill. What he saw was very surprising indeed.

The General seemed to be looking into an ornate mirror hanging on the wall and talking to his own reflection.

Nutty kept looking and as his eyes grew accustomed to the dim light he noted with some surprise that the reflection in the mirror was not the General but a different man and the two men were having a conversation. The squirrel pressed his little ear against the glass of the window and could just about hear what they said. He told the two friends, who were sitting absolutely still, listening to every word:

'The General was talking to someone about finding something and it was really very important to whoever he was talking to in the mirror. They needed to find *the thing* so they could be *reunited* the General said. Whilst they were still talking, some of the General's guards arrived. He'd sent them to Creatown to find Father Rhyme and was furious to hear that he'd disappeared before the guards could capture him. He was really angry with the guards for being so slow and gave one of them a clip around the ear so hard that it sent him flying across the hut. He told them that the next day they needed to go back and find someone who knew where Father Rhyme had gone. Well, the following day they came back and broke camp. I couldn't get close enough to hear what they were saying, but the General looked pretty pleased so I guess they found something out.'

'My goodness,' Relly said. 'Father Rhyme's disappeared. You don't think he's been taken?'

'No, I think he got away,' Ogi Ogi replied. 'We'd better try and find Father Rhyme before the General does.'

The three friends sat around the fire and talked long into the evening. The squirrel had been fascinated by The Prospector's mines and the magic dream stone. He'd asked them to describe their dreams and the meeting with their children three times over. By the time they'd gone to sleep, the moon had been high in the sky and the rain outside had settled down to a gentle pitter-patter. The fire's dim, red glow kept them warm as they slept peacefully.

CHAPTER FIVE

CREATOWN

The two friends woke up to the sound of water dripping from the trees and birds singing. The calls varied from squawks to tweets and there must have been a dozen different types of birds. The friends could hear the squirrel clattering around the clearing whilst they lay dozing.

'I suppose we'd better try and find out what happened to Father Rhyme,' Relly said. 'If the General left here in a hurry, they must have found some clues.'

'Yes,' Ogi Ogi agreed, 'I hope he's escaped. If the General found him, he might know where to find the dream stone. If he's gone to the mines, The Prospector and Small Bear are in danger too!'

Nutty came bounding back into the hut with armfuls of pots and pans. He stormed back out and they could hear more banging and clanging from outside. The door flew open again and the squirrel shot back through the door with a folding chair under one arm, a suitcase under the other, and several bags hanging off various bits of his body. He looked a bit like your mum or dad when they come back from the supermarket and try to carry all the shopping in from the car at once.

'There!' he said, flinging his luggage onto the floor, 'That's the rest of it. I'm moving back in. I'm sick of hiding in the trees. The General and his dullards can come back if they like and I will knock their blocks off with a hazelnut or two.'

'Yes, you can be quite accurate with your nuts when you want to be,' Ogi Ogi laughed and rubbed his head as he remembered how the first time they'd met the squirrel, he'd bombarded them with nuts to keep them out his wood.

'Breakfast, anyone?' the squirrel asked, excitedly.

'Yes please,' replied Relly and Ogi Ogi at the same time.

Nutty had soon prepared a fabulous bowl of hazelnut porridge. It was so rich and creamy that they savoured every last spoonful. Ogi Ogi even turned the bowl upside down and tried to lick all the bits from the edges. Once they'd eaten, they gathered up their things and pulled on their boots.

'Would you like to come with us and see The Prospector's mines?' Relly asked.

'No, I need to stay here and guard my wood,' the squirrel said. 'Hearing how brave you've both been has given me courage. I need to stand up to the bullies.'

The two friends stepped out into the clearing as the bright, shining sun broke through the clouds. The clearing was full of large puddles and Relly couldn't resist it: he ran as fast as possible and took a huge leap into the air, landing with a splash in the middle of the biggest one. Ogi Ogi and the squirrel jumped into the puddles next to him and the three friends spent several minutes splashing and sploshing.

'A rainbow!' the squirrel shouted.

The three stopped jumping up and down and looked at the arc of bright colours that had formed in the clearing.

The splashing had created a mist of water which the sunlight had hit to make a rainbow. Once it had faded, the friends said their goodbyes and Relly and Ogi Ogi headed North, through the woods, towards the town.

At the edge of the woods they came to the path that would lead them back to the road. The ground was soggy and as they walked their feet made loud squelching sounds. It was fun at first and they both started mud-skiing. They would sprint as fast as they could and then jump onto both feet and slide as far as possible. As they skidded along on the mud it splattered up in the air, sometimes they'd trip and land on their bums. But walking in mud is tiring. Every step is a little bit harder because the mud gets stuck to your boots, making your feet heavy. It's only a little bit of extra weight, but it makes a difference.

The two friends had been walking along the main road for just an hour or so, but Relly's little legs had already begun to ache. The second day of walking always seemed worse than the first and the mud was getting thicker. He was starting to wonder just how they'd made it all the way to the Northern Mountains on their last adventure.

'My feet have started to hurt,' Ogi Ogi whimpered. 'And this beret is making my head hot. The feather keeps drooping onto my face and in a minute I'm going to sneeze so hard it will probably blow off.'

'I know,' Relly replied. 'I was just thinking how long it's taking. I'm glad no one is chasing us this time though, like they were when we walked to the Northern Mountains.'

The two friends plodded on through the mud: then Relly had an idea. 'I know, let's sing a marching song. If Glump were here he'd sing us a song and we'd soon be stomping along at a fair old pace. How about this?'

We're marching in the mud, it's splattery, fun and good
We're marching in the mud, onward as we should
We're marching in the mud, it's splattery, fun and good
We're marching in the mud, onward as we should

They marched along singing their song and in what seemed like no time at all, the town came into view. 'Do you think Big George might have stood here when he decided to build the town?' Ogi Ogi asked. Big George had built Creatown. There was a statue of him in the main square. Apart from looking like a boy of about seven or eight and being a tremendous inventor, not much was known about the town's founder.

'He might have done,' Relly replied. 'He must have been very clever to have invented the astrological clock.'

The astrological clock sits at the top of the town hall's tower. It's the tallest building in the town and it can be seen from anywhere. The clock has a sun and moon that orbit the tower on a rail each day, and a magical face that changes its picture according to the seasons. At the base of the clock face lives an old couple whose lives change with the time throughout the day. They can be eating breakfast, sweeping leaves, cutting corn or drinking warm, hot chocolate. Sometimes they decide to have a lie in and this confuses the people of Creatown who see the old couple gently snoring in their bed and assume it is still early morning.

'I bet the dial's changed to Autumn now. The trees have probably started losing their leaves,' Ogi Ogi said.

The two friends hurried through the town until they found Father Rhyme's Shop of Curiosities. They pressed their faces up against the glass and peered into the shop. The curtains were half closed and the windows were dirty so it was hard to see inside and make out the dark shapes. It looked still and lifeless. As their eyes became accustomed to the gloom, they realised that some of the furniture and piles of books had been knocked to the floor Relly tried the door handle but it was firmly locked and wouldn't budge.

'Let's try round the back,' Ogi Ogi suggested.

The two friends cautiously followed the narrow alley to the rear gate which gave access to the rear of the shop. Relly crouched down on all fours and allowed Ogi Ogi to stand on his back so that he could reach to climb over the gate. Once inside he lifted the latch to let Relly in. Slowly and quietly they tiptoed to the door. Whilst the shop seemed deserted, there was a strange, spooky feel about the place. The back door was shut but it looked damaged: one of the panes of glass was smashed and the wood around the lock was splintered. Relly tried the handle and the door didn't move.

'Give it a shove,' Ogi Ogi said. Relly gave it a push and it moved a little. He tried again, harder, but it wouldn't budge further. 'Come on,' said Ogi Ogi. 'I'll help.'

Both friends gave the door a huge shove at the same time. It suddenly came unstuck and they went flying through and tumbled into the kitchen where they sat still as mice while the dust floated up around them. Once they were sure no one had heard the kerfuffle, they stood up, slowly. Relly put his finger to his lips to suggest they be as quiet as possible. Ogi Ogi burped loudly and then jumped up, knocking over a stack of pans as he stood up. A huge iron kettle fell crashing to the floor. Relly and Ogi Ogi looked at each other and then burst into laughter.

Once they'd stopped laughing, they carefully made

their way through the hall into the shop. The shop, like the kitchen, was covered in dust and it was obvious that no one had been there for some time. Relly began by lighting several candles. Despite being daylight outside, the shop windows were so dirty that they let hardly any light in.

'Someone was in here looking for something,' Relly said.

'I bet I know who,' Ogi Ogi replied. 'Let's hope the evil scoundrel didn't find it either. What do you think we're looking for? A key, a book, a map…?'

'I guess it's something written down, because that's what he was good at: words,' Relly said hurriedly. The two friends searched thoroughly for another hour, until they both collapsed into two dusty, old, green chairs either side of the empty fire place.

'Hello,' whispered a voice.

Relly nearly jumped out his chair. 'Hello?' he said. 'Who's there?'

'It's me, Dorothy,' she replied. They'd met Dorothy before, on their way back to the Castle from the Northern Mountains.

Dorothy nervously walked down the stairs. She looked white as a sheet. Relly dashed over and gave her a big hug. 'So nice to see you,' he said. As he hugged her, he could feel her shaking with fear. 'Oh you poor thing,' he said. 'Come and sit down. You look like you've seen a ghost.'

Dorothy took the seat next to Ogi Ogi and gave him a small smile. Her black hair was fastened back from her face in a ponytail and she wore a red dress. 'I'm sorry,' she said, 'I thought the General and his guards had come back to look for Father Rhyme and his book. They were here for two days, tearing the place apart, but I don't think they found anything. I hid in my shop next door. If I went into my kitchen I could hear them talking. They were desperately looking for a book of some sort, but they didn't find it.'

'It must have been important,' said Relly. 'I wonder where the book and Father Rhyme have gone?'

'I don't know,' said Dorothy, 'but not long after you had left to go back to the castle, I found this letter addressed to you both.'

Dorothy handed Relly a crumpled letter, with their names written in beautiful black ink. The letter was sealed with a blob of red wax. He took it out and read it aloud to them:

Dear Boys,

I hope you managed to complete your adventure and find the stone. I fear there is little time left before the darkness closes around us. If you are reading this, then I am gone. So you must learn where I have come from...

> *Hidden somewhere in a nook,*
> *You will find an ancient book.*
> *In it are the notes I took.*
> *Now, off you go and have a look!*

I must go on one last adventure myself now to try and stop the General. I've gone North to find a ship and then I will head to sea.

Find the clues within and then let the adventure begin.

Father Rhyme

'We need to find a book,' said Relly. 'But what's a *nook*?' Ogi Ogi asked.

'I think it's a quiet corner, a corner where people often read or try to do things without being disturbed,' said Relly. 'Let's go and have a look!'

Poor Dorothy felt too tired and shaken to help, so she sat by the fireside and wrapped herself in a blanket. The two friends began searching for the nook. They started in the corners of the shop but didn't find anything. A thick layer of dust had settled across most of the furniture and as they searched dusty clouds puffed up to the ceiling. Relly began to cough as the dust tickled his throat. 'Open the windows,' he spluttered. Ogi Ogi opened the shop doors and used a long pole with a hook at the end to open the high up windows near the ceiling.

After another half an hour of searching, the two friends sat on the floor feeling tired and sad. Relly looked up at the ceiling. The shop's walls were covered in bookcases that were crammed with books. Just above the shop's counter, there was a small balcony with a chair and several filing cabinets. Relly could see a narrow spiral staircase behind the counter, but the entrance was blocked by several piles of books.

'What do you think is up there?' he said.

'Where?' asked Ogi Ogi.

'Up there on the balcony, above the counter where you pay for things.' They began clearing the pile of books which blocked the entrance. Once it was clear, they carefully climbed the stairs and made their way on to the balcony.

The balcony was narrow with a low safety rail to stop Imaginos falling off. A tall bookcase stood against the wall, with hundreds of books neatly arranged in alphabetical order. At the end of the balcony was a small pile covered by a dust sheet. Relly pulled off the sheet to reveal a small writing desk and a chair. Unlike the rest of the room, the desk was free of dust. An inkwell and a quill were neatly arranged in one corner, with a stack of plain paper in the middle.

'Why is there a feather in a pot?' asked Ogi Ogi. 'How curious.'

'It's called a *quill*. It's a goose feather which has had the end sharpened. You dip it in ink to write. It's an old-fashioned type of pen,' Relly explained, with a smile.

Ogi Ogi began searching around the desk.

'Can you see anything?' Relly asked.

'Nothing,' said Ogi Ogi. 'Hang on, what's this under the desk?'

One of the desk's legs was shorter than the other by about ten centimetres. Under the leg there was a thick bound book. On top of the book sat an old iron key on a short length of string. Father Rhyme had worn the key around his neck. Ogi Ogi yelped with excitement and held up the book. 'Look, Relly,' he cried, 'I think I've got it!'

The thick, leather covered book was heavy and they had to be careful when they carried it down the stairs. They placed it on a low table near to the fire and began opening the shop's curtains. Light flooded into the room and they could see more clearly. Whilst they'd been searching the shop, Dorothy had lit the fire and the whole place had begun to look less spooky.

The book was covered in a thick layer of dust and they could see their hand-prints in it. Relly blew the dust away, which caused Ogi Ogi to sneeze loudly and a huge plume of dust shot up into the air. He started coughing and used his beret to try and fan it away. Once they'd cleaned the cover, they read the title: '*Journal of Rhymes and Other Things.*'

They opened the book and began to look through its pages. It was crammed full of notes, riddles, poems and occasional pictures. The journal had dates for each entry.

'It's like a cross between a diary and a book,' Relly said. 'It begins in 1938 and continues right up to a few months ago.'

The three Imaginos sat and read though the first entry in the diary. This was the longest entry in the whole book and talked about Father Rhyme's earliest memories and Fred, the child who had imagined him. It described several years of Fred's childhood with dates underlined in several places. It looked like Father Rhyme had started writing it not long after his changing, when he thought he'd played with Fred for the final time.

Fred had grown up in London. His dad had been a journalist and wrote about the war for a newspaper called *The Telegraph*. His mum was an actress and performed regularly at the *Shepherd's Bush Empire*. He went to the local school and loved reading and writing stories. Books were much rarer then, so he read anything he could find, even boring old newspapers. He particularly enjoyed the books which told of the adventures of the Hardy Boys. But things had changed when the war started. Fred stayed in London for a while, but it wasn't safe because German planes were flying over dropping bombs on the city so he'd been evacuated to the countryside where it was safer.

He had gone to stay on a farm just outside a mining village in Cornwall where he'd lived with a family called the Morgans. The Morgans' father had been called up to fight the Germans, so Mrs Morgan looked after the farm with the help of Old Man Ralph. They had two children, Nancy and Edward, with whom Fred got along very well.

'Bombs?' Ogi Ogi said. 'I wonder what bombs are and who the Germans were.'

'There's a load more here about their adventures on the farm, trips to the beach and something called *the Blitz*,' Relly replied. 'But we don't have time to read the whole diary now. We can read the rest when we've found something that will help us find Father Rhyme. We need to get to him before the General does.'

Relly and Ogi Ogi began leafing through the book. After the Changing when his child had stopped playing with him, Father Rhyme had begun exploring Imago. He spent a year investigating and discovering the Rainbow Rainforest, which was to the West of the Western Mountains. Several small maps charted his journey, with notes describing the things that he'd seen and the Imaginos he'd met. Relly gasped, 'The Rainbow Rainforest sounds fantastic, Ogi Ogi. We must go there one day.' He read out the section describing the rainforest.

At the edge of the Western Mountains, the river tumbles over a huge cliff face and falls down to the forest below. At the base of the waterfall, where the mist of the falling water meets the sun, there is a never-ending rainbow. On a clear day this spreads across the rainforest, making it seem like the trees themselves are alive with colours.

The friends went to the end of the book. Just after the last entry, they found a small note tucked inside the book. Relly pulled the note out and read it aloud.

I've written this book
So take a good look.
Danger clouds the land,
Dark forces at hand,
Secrets hidden within
From the rhymes that do spin.
Read them with care –
You'll find answers there.

The three Imaginos began reading the last entry:

Over the years, I've been on many adventures in this wonderful land. I've climbed the Northern Mountains and walked to the edge to the Eastern Desert. I dare say I've seen and spoken to more Imaginos than any other that's lived. On my adventures, I learned much of Imago's history and the strange days when there was more magic in the land.

> *Long ago when the land was young*
> *Tales were told and songs were sung;*
> *Skies were full of flying lizards;*
> *Many Imaginos were wizards.*
> *There came to be a powerful mage,*
> *A colourful, playful, wonderful sage.*
> *It's said he created three objects of power*
> *Whilst working high up in his tower:*
> *The first, a mirror to make things clear;*
> *The second, crown jewels to be held dear;*
> *The third, a tool to vanquish a ghoul:*
> *Bring them together to defeat any fool.*

Once they'd finished reading, Ogi Ogi turned dark green. 'Three objects of power? What on Earth could they be?' he asked.

Relly rubbed his chin, deep in thought. 'He's listed three objects: a mirror, a crown and a tool. The tool could be used to vanquish a ghoul, so it must be some sort of weapon,' he speculated.

Ogi Ogi's stomach gurgled. 'Do you remember when we were trying to escape from the castle and we went past the

General's rooms? He was talking to someone in a mirror. I bet that's the same mirror, so he's got one of the items already.'

'It might be worse than that,' Relly replied. 'He may have the tool as well: when he fled the Castle he took the mirror and the Sword of Grivadale. If he has two of the items already that only leaves the Crown. In his letter, Father Rhyme said he'd gone North to find a ship. Do you think that has anything to do with the Crown?'

'We'd better look through the journal and find his notes on the Northern Mountains,' Ogi Ogi said.

They began quickly scanning through the journal. But the handwriting was small and the pages were large, so it took some time before they found the chapter on the Northern Mountains. There was a long section describing his adventures there. He had discovered some caverns under the mountains and like Relly and Ogi Ogi in their first adventure, had used these to help reach the summit. There were several maps showing his climb and a poem about the icy winds, but no mention of a Crown.

After I'd explored the Northern Mountains, I headed East. I followed the mountains until they ended. The Eastern Desert lay ahead of me, stretching for miles and miles. The heat was unbearable but I decided to see what lay on the other side of the desert. I made myself a sled to travel on and loaded it with water and supplies, and I headed towards the Needle Tower far to the East. In the middle of the day when it was hottest, I slept under the sled. At night when it was cooler, I pulled it towards the distant landmark.

After ten days, the mountains looked like a grey band of shark's teeth sticking out of the horizon. All I could see was golden sand stretching for miles and miles in every direction. The Needle Tower looked slightly bigger, but it was hard to tell in the heat of the midday sun. At its hottest, the sky seemed to blur if you looked into the distance for too long. The thirst was unbearable. My mouth felt dry all the time and my legs ached constantly. How I wished for Fred to think of me, so I could go to London and hear about the books he'd been reading. But Fred had grown up and he wouldn't be thinking of me again. I felt a deep sadness as I slowly made my way further into the desert. By the fifteenth day, I was beginning to run low on water. I knew I wouldn't die, but each step of the journey was becoming unbearable.

On the twentieth day, there was a sand storm which lasted for two nights. The storm blocked out the sun and it was dark, even during the day. I sheltered under the sled and tried to sleep for as long as possible. Once the storm had passed, I climbed to the top of the nearest sand dune and searched the horizon for the tower. I couldn't see it anywhere. I felt my heart beat faster as I began to panic. Where was I? Was I lost? Then I saw it. It was much bigger now than it had been before, so I must finally be getting closer. I allowed myself an extra ration of water and then set off with new energy.

The tower steadily grew in size as it came closer. The sun climbed higher in the sky and each step got harder. I was finding it difficult to see the tower as I stumbled forward. I reached the top of a large sand dune and it looked like the tower was surrounded by rocks or trees. Then as I skidded down the other side of the dune, it disappeared again. I trudged forward until I reached the

*next dune. As I steadily climbed to the top, I felt like
I had no energy left at all. I tripped as I came over
the top and slid down the other side, face first. When
I looked up, I could see the tower just in front of me.
Then I must have fainted.*

*When I woke up, I thought I must have gone to
Fred's world. I was lying in a hammock surrounded by
trees. The shade of the trees was refreshing after days
in the desert sun. I could hear parrots squawking in the
background and a gentle breeze rocked me from side to
side. Then a smiling Imagino holding a coconut in one
hand, smiled down at me.*

'Oh my goodness!' Relly exclaimed. 'It must have taken
him nearly a month to walk there. His feet must have
swollen up like big, red, clown shoes by the time he
arrived.'

'There are Imaginos across the desert!' Ogi Ogi cried.
'Who'd have thought it! Do you think that's where Father
Rhyme has gone?'

'The letter said North not East so I don't know,' Relly
replied.

'Hee hee hee hee,' came a low chuckle. The three
Imaginos looked around. They'd heard someone laughing
but they couldn't see anyone. Then they heard it again.
'Hee hee hee hee hee hee hee...pssssssssst!'

Relly looked hard at the clock on the mantelpiece
above the fire. Where on Imago was that noise coming
from? When he stared hard at the clock he could just
about make out a face. The hands looked a bit like the
nose and either side of the face, the wooden case had
two carved roses that sort of looked like eyes. As Relly

squinted harder, Mr Nowhere came into sight.

They'd met Mr Nowhere before. He really was the strangest of all Imaginos. He could appear in anything that you might be able to see a face in. Quite often when we look at something, it's possible to see a face. It might be a door handle with two screws for eyes and the keyhole for a mouth, or a pattern on a tree which just looks like a nose and a mouth. Once people have seen a face, then they can imagine a person, and that Imagino is Mr Nowhere. He doesn't have a body, nor does he live in any one place at any one time. When they had first met him, his mischievous smile and sparkling eyes had worried the two friends as he looked like he might try and play a trick at any moment. But he'd tried to help them before so they knew he was a friend, not a foe.

'Mr Nowhere!' Relly said. 'What are you doing here?'

'Well, I thought I'd stop in and see what you two fellows are up to,' Mr Nowhere said. 'I've been all over Imago keeping an eye on things since the General escaped. It makes a change from that cold castle with its draughty corridors.'

'Have you seen Father Rhyme?' they all asked in unison.

'You want to know about the old traveller?' Mr Nowhere replied. 'Well, I can only see things where there's a place for me to appear, so I can't be everywhere. I do know he's heading North and that he wants to cross the Eastern Desert again. The General the searching for him and he's getting closer,' he warned.

'Do you know where he's going or what he's looking for?' Relly asked.

'No idea, but I think you are right. The sword is *the*

tool, so I'd guess he's looking for the crown. I'm planning to play a few tricks on the General and hopefully I can slow him down.'

'The answer must be in his journal,' Relly exclaimed. 'We know he's gone North to get a ship, but we've no idea where that could be. If he wants to cross the Eastern Desert again, it could be beyond that. I've never heard of anyone sailing on the Endless Ocean. But until five minutes ago, we didn't know there were Imaginos in the desert. Perhaps The Prospector knows something or can help us look for him as he knows the North better than anyone. If we take the journal we can try and read it on the way.'

Mr Nowhere winked and then slowly faded back into the clock. Relly and Ogi Ogi quickly gathered their things and packed the book safely into their bag. They asked Dorothy to go to the castle and tell the Council of Imago all their news. If they learned anything more in the Northern Mountains, they promised to send news as soon as they could.

Half an hour later, they were taking the road out of Creatown and heading once more towards the Northern Mountains. Relly was just about to start whistling a tune to help keep them stomping along, when he started feeling a bit funny. He felt a little bit dizzy, then like he was falling down...

CHAPTER SEVEN

A NEW HALL

The school was buzzing. The new sports hall was being opened this morning by the local MP and, best of all, Britain's most successful heptathlete ever, Emma Jones. Jane was super excited about the prospect of seeing Emma and maybe even meeting her. She'd won a gold medal at the last two Olympics and now held the world record for the most points ever collected.

The women's heptathlon is made up of seven events: the 100 metres hurdles, high jump, shot put, 200 metres, long jump, javelin throw and 800 metres. Jane really enjoyed athletics and she'd come first in the sprint at the last sports day. But she hadn't tried all the events in the heptathalon. Last summer she asked her dad to buy her a javelin, but he said it was too dangerous to do at home. She'd tried using the bamboo canes from the runner beans in the garden instead, but one very-long throw went off target and into the veg patch, spearing a marrow and her dad was extremely cross.

'I was going to enter that marrow in the village show, but it's ruined now. It looks like a huge vegetable kebab for the barbeque,' he'd shouted.

Mrs Fowler called the morning register. 'Come along, Class Darwin, it's time to see the new hall. Tuck that shirt in,

Moss,' she called chirpily. 'We want to be the smartest class in the school when we meet gold medallist Emma Jones and our Member of Parliament, Henry Harris-Smyth.'

Jane had made sure she was ready to go as soon as Mrs Fowler asked them to get in line. She grabbed Abby's hand and pulled her towards the door, just beating Mildred Marsh to the front of the queue. Once they'd quietened down, Mrs Fowler led them out of the classroom and through the school. They could hear her humming the National Anthem as she strode along the corridor. They gathered in the playground with every other class in the school. There were twelve lines all facing the new hall, where a small stage had been built for the occasion.

Emma Jones and Henry Harris-Smyth MP were standing on the stage next to Mr Brooke, the headmaster. A large red ribbon hung between two posts in front of the doors to the new sports hall. Emma was so close and her gold medal was dazzling in the sunshine. Jane was delighted. She couldn't believe her hero was here, at St Joan's Primary!

Mr Brooke began by thanking the people that had donated extra funds to help the school raise money for the hall. Next he thanked the two guests for coming to open the hall. As Abby looked on, she thought how different Emma and Henry were. They were like chalk and cheese. Emma looked the picture of health. She was wearing her Great Britain tracksuit and neon pink trainers. Henry was wearing a three-piece tweed suit, which barely contained his expanding waistline. Emma's black hair was neatly arranged and tucked in a bun. Henry had grey hair that looked like an ice cream cone had been splatted on his head sideways. Emma smiled politely and occasionally glanced at

Mr Brooke. Henry had a deep frown and a glum expression. Rather than look at the headmaster, he seemed to be glaring at the photographer who was standing next to the stage.

'It's with great pleasure that I now hand over to our guests to formally open the hall,' Mr Brooke said.

Mr Brooke handed a giant pair of scissors to Henry and Emma. They each held one half of the scissors and made their way off the stage to the ribbon outside the hall. They were about to cut the ribbon when Henry Harris-Smyth snatched the scissors out of Emma's hands. He pushed in front of her and cut the ribbon himself. Abby and Jane gasped but before anyone could say anything, he started bellowing, 'It's with great pleasure, as Member of Parliament for Glanthorm, that I pronounce this hall open. I'm sure the Olympian Ms Jones would agree that such a facility will help you become gold medallists of the future.'

He waved to the cameras then flung open the doors and marched into the hall, his large feet slapping the floor as he stomped in. The whole school looked on in stunned silence. After what seemed like a lifetime, Mr Brookes began clapping and then the crowd joined in. Emma, still smiling, waved to the crowd.

'What a beast,' Jane said. 'Did you see him push Emma out of the way? He was like a fat, greedy toad. He just wanted to make sure he was the only one in the picture for the paper.'

Each class was then led into the new sports hall so they could see it for themselves. The hall had a wonderfully polished floor, covered in all sorts of coloured lines for different sports. Several boys from the class were trying to follow the blue line all around the hall and Mrs Fowler had to round them up like a sheep dog. Once the children were sitting on their mats, they were treated to a display of gymnastics from the Year Five and Year Six pupils. They watched in awe as four girls formed a human pyramid, with one of them standing on top of another girl's head. They dismounted acrobatically and the head teacher led the applause. As he stood up to deliver his final speech to the school, suddenly he went flying across the floor.

'Did you see that?' Jane whispered to Abby.

'What?' Abby replied.

'That toad just tripped up Mr Brooke. He moved his foot and caught him as he walked past and I'm sure I saw him laughing.'

Henry was sitting with a gleeful expression on his face. He was beaming out at the hall without a care in the world. As Abby looked at him, she thought how much he actually looked like a toad as well. He had a wide mouth and his eyes seemed to pop out of his big round face as he became more and more excited.

After Mr Brookes had picked himself up, he brushed himself down and smiled. He gave another short speech then invited the whole school to join him in the lunch hall for tea and cake. At the mention of cake, Henry licked his lips and sat up eagerly. The teachers had asked the children to bring in cake donations and Abby's mum had spent all last week baking.

'I hope I get some of my mum's Victoria sponge,' Abby said. 'She makes the most fantastic cakes. We used the jam my dad made after we went raspberry picking in the summer. It's scrumdiddlyumciously yummy.'

'We'd better make sure we are near the front of the queue then,' Jane replied.

They didn't need to worry too much. It looked like

Mrs Fowler wanted her pick of the cakes as well. They were one of the first classes to make it to the lunch hall and there were hundreds of different cakes left. The children were allowed one glass of squash and one slice of cake each. To Abby and Jane's delight, they asked for Victoria sponge and were given a choice from three different types. Abby proudly pointed to the one her mum had made and winked at Jane. The cake was delicious. They both made happy noises as they ate it slowly, savouring each mouthful.

'Eating this reminds me of the exploding cake,' Jane said.

Last term, before Mrs Fowler had seen the error of her ways, she'd made the children bake a cake in the school's kitchens. Jane had been playing with Ogi Ogi, when he accidentally dropped a tub of baking powder into the mixture. The cake became so enormous that it ended up exploding out of the oven all over the children and the hall.

'Oh yes,' laughed Abby. 'That was jolly funny. Do you remember the cake dripping off Mrs Fowler's face? It's a shame Relly was in Imago and didn't see it as well. I bet he'd have loved to have seen Ogi Ogi dance around the top of the mixing bowl.'

'I wonder what Relly and Ogi Ogi are up to now,' Jane replied. 'It's amazing to think that they live in their own world and can have adventures of their own when we aren't playing with them.'

Abby began thinking about Relly and imagined him looking at all the cakes and trying to pick his favourite one. She looked over at the cake table and pictured him dancing in between the battenberg and the fairy cakes.

Suddenly a large shadow loomed over them: 'What's that, little girl?' asked a rather plump and pompous looking

Henry Harris-Smyth. 'Who are Relly and Ogi Ogi? I must say they do sound like interesting characters.' He smiled at them showing a row of yellow teeth and then moved closer making them both feel a little scared.

'They're our imaginary friends,' Abby replied.

'Oh marvellous! I would have thought children these days would be more interested in playing on their electronic slabs or watching TV. You must be very clever,' he said in a patronising way. He then smirked at them and took a large, slurpy swig of tea before continuing to talk at them.

'I had an imaginary friend when I was about your age. He was a fabulous companion. We spent hours playing soldiers and building forts. Not like children these days. No, we played proper games. Well I bet you two girls are enjoying some time off lessons eh?'

With that he shoved an enormous piece of cake between his big fat rubbery lips and started chewing with his mouth open. Jane thought he looked like a sort of pudding mixer with bits of mashed up cake tumbling around in his mouth.

'Yes, Sir,' Abby said politely. She thought he was very rude and didn't like the way he was speaking to her as if she were just a baby.

'So tell me about these friends...where do they live?' he asked.

Abby was starting to worry. This all seemed a bit odd. She gave Jane a sideways glance. Jane looked totally bamboozled. She was staring up at the great toad as he loaded more cake into his mouth. She looked like she'd been hypnotised by him.

'They live in Imago,' she replied. 'It's where our imaginary friends live when they aren't playing with us, Sir.'

Jane was delighted Abby had spoken to The Toad. She

was a little bit shy and found it hard to talk to new people anyway. But Henry Harris-Smyth was the most odious man she'd ever met. She was speechless and couldn't stop staring at his red face and strange cone-shaped hair.

'Sounds splendid,' he said. 'I'd really like to hear more about this Imago place.'

Abby didn't really want to tell him any more about Imago or their imaginary friends. Instead she noticed that he'd run out of cake and decided to try and change the subject. 'Would you like some more cake, Sir?' she asked.

'Oh yes, bravo,' replied Henry without so much as a please or thank you.

She quickly dashed off to the cake table and began searching for the worst looking piece of cake. Relly was delighted to help. He went from plate to plate and began sniffing the cakes. He suddenly stopped and began jumping up and down and waving his arms in the air. Abby found him next to a plate of coffee and walnut cake. There was quite a lot of it left as children aren't generally keen on coffee flavoured cake. Sitting on top of the largest piece of cake was a huge wasp. Relly was pointing at it and flapping his arms. Abby carefully placed the piece of cake on the plate and slowly walked back to Henry and Jane.

'Here you go, Sir,' said Abby, passing him the cake.

Before he could reply, Mrs Fowler came waltzing across the hall and stood directly in front of him. She smiled at the girls and then turned to the MP. The girls both breathed a huge sigh of relief. It looked like they weren't going to have to speak to him any more. Then a strange thing happened. Mrs Fowler, who was now one of the most pleasant teachers you could ever meet, fixed her powerful stare upon the MP. Before the last adventure she had been known as 'The Fowl One', because she looked a bit like a scrawny chicken and she'd been so mean. She'd been known to use her hypnotic gaze to knock children out. The girls looked at her and thought that her blue eyes seemed to swirl as she stared at the horrible MP.

Henry Harris-Smyth had been having a fine time eating as much cake as possible when he'd met these two children. He'd been thinking about how he could probably take the afternoon off if this went on any longer, as there wouldn't be time to get back to his office today. But then they'd started speaking about Imago and just when he was about to find out what they knew about this place, a wiry old teacher had got in his way and started staring at him. Her gaze seemed to be boring into him and she smiled as she moved closer. The whole thing was starting to make him feel a bit sick. The cake in his tummy started to churn around and he had a feeling he might need a bathroom rather quickly.

After a long pause she introduced herself, 'Mrs Fowler,' she said to him, with an icy smile.

'Delighted I'm sure,' he replied.

He picked up the coffee and walnut cake and began to take a bite. Just as he was about to chomp into it he noticed the huge wasp. He dropped the cake and jumped backwards. The strange old teacher was still smiling at him and he was sure her eyes had started to glow.

'Errr, terribly sorry about that,' he said. 'You must excuse me madam, I'm feeling a little queasy. I must find the nearest toilet.'

'Just to the right of the entrance,' she said.

The two girls looked at Mrs Fowler as the MP headed off to find the toilet. She turned and gave them a wink and then marched off towards the tea and cake.

'How about that then?' said Abby.

'She was brilliant,' Jane said. 'She used her super swirling stare on him. I wonder if she still carries round those awful smelling salts she used to try and use on children if they fainted. That stuffy old toad deserved a dose of those pongy crystals.'

The two girls began giggling and joined in with a game of team tag that Tom Clark had started. They soon forgot about Henry Harris-Smyth as they dashed around the hall. After another half an hour, the bell rang and each teacher gathered up their class and led them out of the hall.

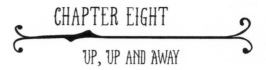

CHAPTER EIGHT

UP, UP AND AWAY

Once the General had fled the castle, Father Rhyme knew that he needed to leave Creatown fast. He knew the General would come for him once he heard about the quest he'd sent Relly and Ogi Ogi on. He'd known instantly where he needed to go. He must cross the Eastern Desert once more and stop the General becoming any more powerful. But how could he walk all that way again? It was hard enough when he was a young Imagino but now his bones creaked in the morning and he slept most afternoons. He hadn't walked more than a mile in the last ten years, let alone a hundred. So, just as Relly and Ogi Ogi had finished their last adventure, Father Rhyme began his own. He started by heading for the toadstool village. He knew he needed to leave Creatown without being seen, so he'd hidden under a pile of hay on the back of a rickety old cart. He'd climbed in and covered himself over. While he waited to leave, he'd stayed as still as a mouse and tried not to let the itchy hay make him sneeze. After a long afternoon on the bumpy road, the cart had stopped at the fork in the road between Waterly Hole and Mushroontan. The Imagino driving the cart had gone off with a bucket to fetch some water for his donkey and whilst he was away, Father Rhyme had slowly lowered himself down from the cart and hidden in the field next to the road. After the cart had left, he waited to make sure the road was clear and once he was sure it was safe, he turned left at the fork and slowly made his way to Mushroontan.

The village of Mushroontan was very old, with twelve toadstool shaped houses and a deep wishing well at its centre. Father Rhyme knew that a very gifted seamstress lived in the village and he hoped that she'd be able to help him with his plan to cross the desert.

His child Fred had always been fascinated by flying. He'd loved the series of Biggles books about a young pilot who joined the Royal Flying Corps and flew planes in the war. Fred dreamed of being a pilot one day and spent many hours imagining himself flying through the skies. But he needed a co-pilot and so, in Fred's imagination, Father Rhyme had become an explorer of the skies as well. During these adventures he'd learned all about airplanes, airships and balloons. They'd built a balloon together using a pillow case, some coat hangers and a small basket. It was this memory which had given Father Rhyme the idea to build a balloon to try and cross the desert. He slowly walked into the village and headed towards a group of Imaginos standing by the well. As he approached, a colourful looking Imagino turned to him.

'Owight there, me old pot and pan?' May said. 'Why don't ya come over here and sit yourself down.'

May was a mishmash patchwork doll made up of hundreds of tiny pieces of material and looked scruffy most of the time. Her hair was made out of tufts of wool of different lengths and colours and she had large, odd-sized buttons for eyes.

'Pot and pan?' Father Rhyme replied. He was completely confuddled. Nobody had ever referred to him as a pot and pan.

'Sorry me old china, pot and pan means "old man",' May said.

'China?' Father Rhyme replied looking confused.

'"China plate" means "mate",' May said. 'I'm sorry, fella, I'm a Cockney so I talk in what they call *Rhyming Slang* most of the time. It sounds like another language. There's a whole dictionary of cockney rhyming slang. It was used in the olden days so other people couldn't understand what we was talking about. Like a secret language. We change some of the words for other words that rhyme with 'em. So *old man* becomes *pot and pan*. I will try to talk proper then so you don't get too confused.'

'What's a cockney?' asked Father Rhyme.

'Anyone who was born in London within earshot of the Bow bells,' explained May.

Father Rhyme was absolutely fascinated. He'd never heard of a rhyming language other than his own. He wanted to hear more about it. Where had it come from? How many people spoke it? Perhaps it was something he could learn more about and study but he really needed to find the seamstress.

Well I often speak in rhyme, my dear
But I'm afraid the meaning is not always clear
I'm seeking a seamstress who maybe lives here
And I'm going to need some help, I fear

Once he'd finished talking, he smiled and stroked his long grey beard.

'That'd be Pearl,' exclaimed May. 'She's a wizard with a needle, there's nothing she can't make or create,' she continued. 'Why, me chalk farm, I mean…me arm…was practically hangin' off the otha day, but she sewed it back on good as new. I'm sure she can help you out. What's your name, me old china?'

'I'm Father Rhyme,' he replied.

'Rhyme!' she said guffawing with laughter and stamping her foot.

Pearl lived in toadstool number one. Her child had loved to make clothes for her dolls and teddies. She could crochet, knit, sew, weave and embroider and her best friend May kept her company while she worked. Pearl looked like a beautiful child's doll. She was made of a rich blue fabric that felt like silk to touch. She had large, pearl buttons for eyes and a shiny penny for a nose. She could make anything from a few scraps of material and some thread. Her skills were often in demand with many Imaginos calling on her for repairs to clothes or even themselves.

May and Pearl were good friends but they looked and sounded completely different. Whilst Pearl sounded like the Queen of England when she spoke, May sounded like a true cockney. May lived at toadstool number four. She had come back from the Princess's dungeons in a terrible state and had needed most of her seams re-sewing and the stuffing replaced in one of her legs.

May led Father Rhyme through the village to Pearl's home. All the toadstool houses had coloured roofs, each with different coloured spots. Number one had purple spots and a chimney stack that was painted a dark green, making it look as if a large caterpillar was sticking out of the top. The door was purple too and had a large brass knocker in the shape of a dog. The sound of operatic singing could be heard faintly from inside the house.

May firmly grabbed the knocker and rapped on the door four times. On the fourth knock she delayed slightly. 'Knock, knock, knock...knock.' 'That's so she knows it's me, see? If it's someone selling summat, they won't do my special knock,' she said winking at him cheekily.

After a few minutes Pearl appeared at the door with a beaming smile. 'Good morning my dear,' she said to May. She then paused and looked at Father Rhyme over the top of her glasses. 'Pleased to make your acquaintance, Sir. I'm Pearl,' she said.

> *Hello, My Dear, I'm Father Rhyme*
> *I speak in verse nearly all the time*
> *I'm looking for a good seamstress*
> *To help me escape a tangled mess*

Once he'd replied he smiled nervously, 'I've been told that a talented Imagino lives in the village and I could do with her help.'

'Is that right?' Pearl smiled. 'Why don't you both come in rather than cluttering up the step. It's wonderful timing because the kettle has just boiled and the tea is brewing. If we go through to the sitting room, you can tell me more about what brings you to my door.'

Pearl led them into her sitting room where there were several large chairs, each covered with beautiful tapestry material showing different types of birds. In the centre of the room sat a low table holding an enormous basket filled with knitting stuff. There were knitting needles of all different shapes and sizes, multi-coloured balls of wool and what appeared to be a half-knitted jumper. Once they'd sat down, Pearl scurried back and forth between the kitchen and sitting room bringing back a fresh pot of tea, cups, several plates and a cake stand containing scones filled with a rich raspberry jam and cream. She carefully set out the cups and then carefully poured the tea. The cups were made of a bone china so beautifully patterned with small, pink roses and so delicate that when Father Rhyme held his up to the window he could see the light through it.

'So, my dear man, why do you need my help?' Pearl asked.

Father Rhyme started by telling them about his escape from the General. He had to try hard not to speak in rhyme all the time otherwise it would take hours to tell them his tale. The General had been chasing him, because he'd helped a couple of brave young Imaginos on a quest to save their friend Glump from Princess Marjorie's dungeons. Father Rhyme gave them a poem which explained where they needed to go to find the magic stone that would help them speak to their children. The General wanted anything that would give him more power and Father Rhyme needed to travel far to the East to stop him getting hold of the final piece to the jigsaw.

His story was interrupted by a massive 'Slllllurrrpppp!'

May's fascinated eyes watched him intently as she peered at Father Rhyme over her saucer whilst slurping her tea from it. 'I met that Glump while he was doin' bird. Sorry I mean "in prison". He's a lovely big green fella, full o' stories he was. His friends stayed in my toadstool on their way to the Northern Mountains as well. Ever so neat they was. Tidied me 'ouse for me an everyfin,' May said.

May kept slurping her tea whilst Pearl delicately sipped hers from the cup. During the time he'd been speaking, May had messily eaten two scones whereas Pearl had only genteelly nibbled at hers.

'I'm here because I need your help to build a balloon to help me travel across the Eastern Desert,' Father Rhyme said. 'I need a seamstress to help me sew a huge air balloon which I can fill with hot air and then float across the desert to the far off tower. A long time ago I walked there but I'm afraid I couldn't even walk all the way here on my own, let alone across half the length of Imago. Are you able to help me with the balloon?'

Pearl set down her tea. 'I'd be delighted,' she replied. 'That sounds like a wonderful thing to make but we are going to need a lot of material and it will take at least a week.'

'Oh dear,' muttered Father Rhyme.

'Whatever's the matter?' asked May.

From the General I only just managed to flee
I'm worried that he will come looking for me
His band of guards is sure to come
So I can't linger here, I must continue to run

'Dontch ya worry about a thing me old, mukka,' said May. 'After doin' me time in prison, at 'er Majesty's pleasure, you may say, I decided to make a few improvements to toadstool number four. I've installed a hidden cupboard in the cellar. If they come a-lookin', then we'll stick ya down there and as long as ya don't make a peep, then they won't find ya. You can stay with me while Pearl 'ere is making the balloon.'

Oh thank-you, that's so very kind
I've drawn some plans, if you don't mind

He reached slowly into his pocket and handed Pearl a large piece of folded paper. She cleared the tea and scones from the table and opened the paper out. The plans were drawn neatly with precise measurements to show how large the pieces of material needed to be and how they had to be cut to make sure the balloon was the right shape. Pearl placed a pair of half-moon glasses on the end of her nose and stared intently at the plans. After several minutes she took her glasses off and smiled.

'Right then, my friends,' she said. 'We are going to need at least ten duvet covers and as many wire coat hangers as you can find. We will need the coat hangers to make a loose frame to fit the material around.'

She took them through to her small workshop that had been added to the side of the toadstool as a small extension. It was built out of wooden logs and from a distance it looked like it was made of chocolate fingers. Pearl went upstairs and returned with two duvet covers which she immediately began to unpick.

'Come along, come along, the sooner we start the sooner we finish,' Pearl said, her nimble fingers flying along the seams. She shooed them out of the back door and began singing to herself.

May took Father Rhyme back to her toadstool. She gave him a tour of her home, telling him in an excited voice all about various treasured objects and where they'd come from or who had given them to her. 'This 'ere fruit bowl was made by Finnytobbin who lives at number nine. He's got a wonderful way o' makin' things out of clay.

Bakes 'em in a big oven and paints 'em, 'e does.'

She showed him the steps down to the cellar and the secret cupboard she'd added under the stairs. It looked like solid wood, but when Father Rhyme pushed one of the panels in the bottom left hand corner, it sprung open to reveal a narrow gap which would make a very safe hiding place.

'If we try and get some bo-peep downstairs, sorry I mean sleep not bo-peep, we can be near to the cellar in case that wicked General comes a-knocking at night,' May said. 'Right, me old china I'm off to gather up bits and bobs for this balloon. You put your feet up while I see how many duvets and coat hangers I can collect. I'll give toadstool number eight a miss. Timothy Teapot lives there and he ain't right. He's a wrongun and that's for sure. I wouldn't be surprised if he weren't one of the General's spies. I might tell 'im a few porky pies! Why that rhymed, I'm getting the 'ang of this rhyming malarkey.'

'Porky pies?' said Father Rhyme.

'Lies,' May called, as she skipped away chortling to herself.

Father Rhyme settled back into one of her chairs and let his eyes gently close. It had been quite a busy day already and he wasn't used to so much hustle and bustle. He was soon asleep and snoring quietly. As he slept, he began to dream about floating in the blue sky of Imago in a wonderful hot air balloon with his child Fred.

It was much later when May came home carrying a huge bundle of duvets and a basket crammed full of hangers, the toadstool door banging shut behind her. Father Rhyme woke with a start. He rubbed his eyes sleepily and watched as May dropped the basket onto the kitchen table and flung the duvets onto the floor.

'There you go,' she said, triumphantly. 'Pearl will have more than enough to make that flying ship o' yours.' She sat down in the chair next to Father Rhyme and plonked her feet onto a foot stool. She kicked off her boots to reveal her feet clad in old, woolly socks, so worn that her toes were poking through the ends.

'I came up with a fabulous Jackie Chan while I was out looking for material,' May said.

Father Rhyme gave her a confused look. She was talking in riddles again and at first he had no idea what a 'Jackie Chan' was.

'Ah,' he said, thoughtfully, 'I assume you mean "plan".'

'Oh sorry, yes, plan,' May laughed. 'I came up with a cracking plan while I was out. I went to see that rotter Timothy Teapot and told him some porkies (pork pies: lies). Spun him a right old tale, I did. I hid all the duvets first and then I popped by all casual like. "Hello Timothy", I says, "Nice to see you". He invites me in then, he does, because he's nosey as a parker that one. So in I goes and he's all like "Would you like some tea May, so nice to see you, let me read the leaves for you". So I lets him. You see he reads people's fortunes by looking at the tea leaves left in the bottom of the cup after they drunk it. It's a load of rot if you ask me, but he uses it to be all meddlesome and find out what you've been up to. I told him all about you, I did.'

Father Rhyme turned pale and his voice quivered slightly as he said:

What I most fear
Is folk knowing I'm here
I really must flee
Before he finds me

'Keep your beard on, he thinks you're long gone,' May replied beaming, 'I told him you came by earlier and had a drink from the well. He thinks you are on your way to the Rainbow Rainforest to find some treasure. If he is talking to the General, then that trout-faced numpty will be waist deep wading through wet ferns before you know it.

May went on to tell Father Rhyme all about Timothy Teapot. You might think that he would look like a teapot with a name like that but he doesn't at all. His child had loved tea parties and regularly held fabulous, grand affairs with her teddies, dolls and Imagino Timothy. Timothy looked like a boy and he was always very smartly dressed. He had a three-piece, pin striped suit and a smart spotted bow tie. His hair was neatly parted in the middle and he wore shiny black and white shoes. He looked neat and tidy all the time and enjoyed pointing out how scruffy the other Imaginos were. In fact he felt he was terribly important, which made him incredibly annoying. He was an expert at making a pot of tea and hosting parties with light, springy sponge cakes and delicately-cut cucumber sandwiches. He was always inviting others around to join him for tea but more often than not they made their excuses and Timothy was left to eat his tasty party food by himself. Even a delicious cup of tea wasn't worth several hours of Timothy's pompous wittering. But if you did join him for tea, he would always tell your fortune at the end. Just like a fortune teller at a fair, he would wait till the cup was almost empty, then carefully swirl it round three times before quickly tipping out the remaining tea leaving large tealeaves sticking to the sides of the cup. To anyone else looking into the cup, the leaves looked nothing more than black shadowy shapes, but to Timothy they showed objects, people and places and by studying them he was able to put together a story of what might happen in the future. Or so he liked to make people believe.

Father Rhyme was fascinated;

To see the future in tea
How strange this must be
Did the leaves show to you
Things you think might come true?

'It's all a load of codswallop,' May replied. 'He's just using it to be a nosey parker. I'd already told him that I'd met an old Imagino and then when he read my tea leaves he predicted I'd meet a traveller. I said "Oh that must be that old rhyme fella, he was off to the Rainbow Rainforest". He looked real pleased with 'imself then, he did, rubbing his little hands with glee. Why, I should have tipped me cup o' tea right over his 'ead.'

This made them both chuckle and they settled down to a pleasant evening by the fire, smoking fossy moss and talking about adventures they'd shared with their own children. After an hour or two, Father Rhyme drifted off to sleep. He wasn't used to this much activity or excitement. At home he'd got used to having a long nap each afternoon but on his journey he hadn't stopped for days.

The following morning, they were woken up by a loud banging on the door. Father Rhyme's beard was sticking up in the air and he had to quickly pat it down so he could see what was going on. The knocking sounded like a giant stamping its foot.

'Open up! Open up! We're here for the treacherous old fool,' came the cry.

May quickly hauled Father Rhyme out of the chair and

took him down to the hiding place under the stairs. She popped the panel open and slid him in. She put her finger up to her lips and winked, then she carefully shut the door and hurried back up the stairs.

She opened the front door just as one of the guards tried to charge it down. He'd taken a huge run up in an attempt to shoulder barge it open. As May opened the door, he came running through and crashed head first into a wall. He stopped and then started swaying, before collapsing on the floor in a heap.

'You!' a guard cried.

'Me?' May replied. 'What do you smelly toad warts want and why are you trying to break into my home?'

'We want to find the dangerous criminal known as Father Rhyme. He plotted against the throne and is now wanted for his crimes.'

'I heard that the throne's gone and there ain't no Princess, you useless lump. Who are you and what gives you the right to break into my toadstool?' May said.

'I am Lieutenant Lundy, madam and I have orders from the General himself. Plotters have taken the throne back and bewitched the Princess. It is my job to bring them to justice, so stand clear if you don't want this place broken apart,' Lundy replied.

'I can see you've only got 'alf a brain. You're a few spanners short of a tool box if you believe that the General's in the right. He's a tea leaf, I mean thief. He tried to steal the throne. But you take a peak, I've got nowt to hide and I don't want me home torn apart. I met the old fella yesterday, I did. Said he was off to the rainforest,' May replied.

Lundy and another guard searched May's toadstool

from top to bottom. They spent ages searching the rooms upstairs. While they searched, May followed them round and heckled them. She said helpful things like: 'You should look under the bed, plenty of room under there,' or 'oh that wardrobe's huge, you could get two Imaginos in there, me old china.'

After they'd finished, Lundy began pacing around the living room. He then walked straight up to May and lent in as close as possible, so his nose was almost touching hers and she could smell his fishy breath.

'If I find out you are lying to me, I will come back here and unpick you a stitch at a time and pull all your stuffing out. Do you understand me?' he snapped.

May just smiled back at him peacefully, whilst trying not to breathe in. Lundy picked up the guard who'd knocked himself out and carried him out of the toadstool. As they were leaving, May waved cheerily and shouted, 'Laters, potatoes.'

She waited until they'd left the village and then she let Father Rhyme out.

'I told ya me Jackie Chan would work and it did, like a treat. Thick as two short planks that Lundy clout,' she said. 'Right then, now we've got rid of them, let's see how Pearl's doin.'

CHAPTER NINE

THE GENERAL

The General sat on a rock whilst studying a map, deep in thought. He'd been searching for Father Rhyme for weeks yet was still no closer. He knew those two meddlesome Imaginos had been to see the old man before they broke the General's spell over Princess Marjorie. His spies had told him some of the story. It seemed that the hermit (known to his friends as 'The Prospector') that lived in the mountains had some sort of magic stone that he'd given to the two Imaginos. They'd used this to find Marjorie's adult and remind her of her long-lost friend. Once the Princess had played with her adult again, the wicked General had lost control over her and was forced to flee the castle. How he'd like to find them and teach them a lesson. As he imagined them locked in a cold, wet, smelly dungeon, he smiled.

'Erm, Sir?' interrupted Lundy.

The General wasn't listening to his Second in Command. He was still brooding. After his Captain had been captured and slung into the dungeons, he'd had to promote his first Lieutenant, Lundy, to Second in Command. This clot was even more annoying than that nincompoop Captain. At least the Captain hadn't had sufficient brains or imagination to question his orders whereas his blithering fool was always full of questions. Before he answered, he noticed a small beetle scurrying past his foot. He quickly tried to stamp on it, but missed. His day was going from bad to worse.

'What is it?' barked the General.

'Sir, I've been thinking,' said Lundy slowly.

'I doubt that,' the General replied.

'Well, I think we should be chasing the hermit, not Father Rhyme. He's got the stone and that's what those two Imaginos used to free the Princess,' Lundy said.

The General glared at Lundy and clenched his fists his face turning bright red like a beetroot. 'You idiot!' he snapped. 'If that old codger knows about the stone, then he knows about all the magical objects in Imago. The hermit's only interested in shiny things that sparkle, that's why he's spent his whole life under that mountain digging up gems and gold. I'm surprised he doesn't look like a mole by now. No, we need Father Rhyme because he knows more about Imago than any other Imagino. My spies tell me that he travelled all over Imago in his youth. He's been to the farthest reaches of the land and I want to know what he knows. I will screw his thumbs down until he tells me. What I want to know is, why haven't we caught him yet? He's about a hundred years old so he can't be moving very fast, can he?'

Lundy quivered under the General's harsh stare as he also wondered how long it would take to catch one old man.

The General and his troops had spent two weeks searching for Father Rhyme. At first they'd camped in some woods not far from the castle, but they'd had to move. The castle guards had started searching for the

General's soldiers and they'd been chased North towards the Toadstool village. Lundy and his platoon had searched the village, but they'd not found anything. One of his spies reported back that although the old fool had been there he'd left a few days before and was heading west. Lundy and his men had travelled into the Rainbow Rainforest and after several wet, hot days, hacking their way through thick trees and mangroves, the news of a sighting reached them. One of the General's spies had seen Father Rhyme heading North towards the mountains. So they abandoned their search of the Rainbow Rainforest and searched the hermit's run-down cottage instead but there was no sign of anyone having been there recently. He'd ordered his troops to start searching further into the mountains, but there was no sign there of anyone at all.

'Perhaps the hermit's hiding the old Imagino, Sir,' Lundy said.

'We've got no chance of finding that meddlesome miner,' the General replied gruffly. 'I've been trying to catch him for years and he just disappears. He's like a rabbit. You chase him around and then he bolts down his hole. Vermin, that's what rabbits are, and that's what he is.' As he said the word vermin, he started to bash his fist on the rock. 'We need to find him and feed him to that giant bird. They eat rabbits, don't they?'

'Yes, Sir,' Lundy replied.

'If we don't find him today we need to move deeper into the mines and start looking there,' the General said. 'Tell the troops there's no lunch today. I want them to keep searching until they find some clues.'

The General stood up sharply, and stormed back towards The Prospector's cottage. He stormed in, kicking the door as hard as he could. They'd searched the place repeatedly, but he'd decided to have one more look. Whilst he searched through The Prospector's possessions, he cheered himself up by breaking and damaging as many things as possible. He picked up a stool and smashed it on the top of a large wooden table. The stool shattered into bits and he used a leg to smash a cuckoo clock which was hanging on the wall. As it hit the floor, several cogs and springs fell out from the back and it made a funny 'poiiii-iigggging' noise. He was just about to whack it to see if it would poing again when he noticed a small, leather-bound book hidden in the back of the clock. He pulled it out eagerly and began flicking through it.

Busyness Log and Journal

12/03/2003, found three rubies of low quality.

Had to hack the rubies out with a pick from a tunnel under the peak of the Pen y Gaf mountain. There doesn't seem to be much more in the way of gemstones.

18/03/2003, traded quart of gold nuggets with Primrose Dollet of Treeton.

21/03/2003, three quarts of silver mined from a vein in lower tunnels.

The lower tunnels are full of silver. Able to access with a pickaxe, but a few sticks of dynamite would help open up the seam.'

The General smiled. His day was getting better. He'd found the hermit's accounts, which also had a list of all his treasure. Now he'd know precisely what the wrinkly old duffer had found. He flicked backwards and forwards until he found what he was looking for.

15/03/1984, discovered a smooth gem stone the size of a fist in Dragon's Cavern. I've not seen anything like it before. Its milky-white surface seems to swirl as you look at it.

There was another note written next to the entry and this one had been added at a later date with a different pen.

Had the strangest dream last night. It felt like I was speaking to James. I'm sure that the stone had something to do with it. In the evening it seemed to be glowing in the light of the moon. I'm going to lock it away safely until I find out more about it. <u>Not to be sold.</u>

'Cuckoo! Cuckoo! Cuckoo!' chirped the clock.

The General looked down at it. How dare the cuckoo pop out and disturb him. He'd smashed that clock once already. As he stared down at the clock, he thought he noticed a face. He squinted slightly and there he could see it. The hands looked like the nose and the case had two wooden carved swirls that looked like eyes. It was Mr Nowhere and the General was not pleased to see him.

'What are you doing outside the Castle, you bodiless buffoon,' he barked.

'I need entertaining and I wouldn't want you to forget me,' Mr Nowhere replied. 'You came so close to Father Rhyme but you couldn't see what was under your nose all along. Hee hee hee hee.'

'What are you on about you, floating fool?' said the General.

'He was never in the Rainforest. You spent weeks hacking down jungle and being bitten by mosquitoes for nothing,' said Mr Nowhere. 'You are as stupid as that dimwit Captain of yours. You couldn't find a pink elephant in a field with a big sign next to it saying "Pink elephant here!" Why don't you head to the tunnels in the Northern Mountains quickly before you lose him for ever?'

The General felt a huge surge of rage. Mr Nowhere used to stalk him in the castle. He'd appear in objects and make fun of him or tell him things that weren't true. One day he'd tricked the General into following him around the castle for hours. In fact the General was so angry that he ordered his guards to destroy every item Mr Nowhere had ever appeared in so he could never use it again. He picked up the stool leg and marched over to the cuckoo clock.

'This is the last I will hear from you today, you meddling fool,' he said and began whacking the clock over and over again, until it was smashed into hundreds of tiny pieces. He was red in the face and frothing at the mouth by the time he'd finished and looked like an angry pig that was just about to be roasted on a spit.

Father Rhyme was sitting nervously in the basket of the balloon, which had taken several weeks to make. The basket was made by screwing together several delivery crates. And Father Rhyme thought it looked like a rickety old box that he wasn't sure would make the journey across the desert. Finnytobbin, who had made the basket, was quite offended and assured the old man that it certainly wouldn't fall apart because he'd put extra screws in all the right places.

The oil lamp Father Rhyme had borrowed from Pearl was burning nicely and the balloon was slowly filling with hot air. As the warm air blew inside, the material began to billow and dance before taking shape. It looked like a wonderful, multi-coloured ball. A stab of fear flashed through his whole body as he felt the first jolt when the basket started to lift off the ground. Father Rhyme thought about his child Fred and how the boy would have loved to fly off on an adventure in this balloon. If Fred were here, he'd have felt a lot less nervous about the journey ahead.

'Here's a basket of food and a flask of tea,' Pearl said.

'It's been a pleasure, me old china. Come see us when you've crossed the desert and found the missing treasure,' May chirped. 'Make sure you keep your mince pies open while you're up there. You might be able to see where that rotter the General has got to.'

> *Your kindness, my dears*
> *Has moved me to tears*
> *But I must say goodbye*
> *For it's time I should fly!*

Finnytobbin untied the balloon and it began to rise into the air. Father Rhyme waved to the villagers as the balloon drifted upwards. Mushroontan became smaller and smaller as he took to the skies. He could still see his friends waving, but they looked more like ants now as he climbed higher and higher. He peered over the edge of the basket and could see the whole of Imago spread below him. He felt an enormous surge of happiness as the wind ruffled his hair. To the left the Northern Mountains filled the horizon and to the East the green fields below eventually gave way to the Eastern desert. The balloon gathered speed as the wind began to blow him along.

He passed over the road to the mountains and drifted towards The Prospector's cottage. He could see several guards gathered around the cottage. As he floated higher, they started to look like little toy soldiers.

Far below, Lundy had spotted a mysterious flying object and he called the General. 'Sir, Sir, come quick,' Lundy yelled. 'It's a marvel, Sir, I ain't ever seen anything like it!'

The General put the book down and strode out of the cottage. He looked up to where Lundy was pointing and Father Rhyme could see at once that the General had spotted him. Suddenly Father Rhyme realised that the balloon had stopped rising. To his relief he couldn't see any rips in the balloon's fabric but then he saw that the oil lamp had gone out. He needed to relight it quickly before he sank to the ground, or the General would catch him.

'What the devil is that?' Lundy asked.

'It's a hot air balloon,' the General replied.

He stared up at the huge balloon for some time. It was hard to see, but if he squinted he could just about see a basket with an Imagino controlling a small fire underneath it. It could have been the light of the sun, but the General thought that he could see an Imagino with grey hair and then he realised it was Father Rhyme! He stuffed The Prospector's busy-ness log into his pocket.

'Pack up your things immediately!' he screamed at his band of rogues. 'Find as many horses or donkeys as possible. We're going to catch that balloon!'

CHAPTER TEN

BACK TO THE MOUNTAINS

Relly and Ogi Ogi had made good time on their walk North. The weather had been fair and they would only need to walk for another half a day before reaching The Prospector's cottage. The previous night Relly had pitched a little tent in a field by the edge of a wood whilst Ogi Ogi made a small fire. The warmth from the dancing flames turned their cheeks pink as they sat close to read more of the Book of Rhymes in the bright, glowing light.

They searched through the journal until they found the entry that described Father Rhyme's journey across the Eastern Desert. He'd collapsed with exhaustion at the end of his journey and woken up at an oasis.

'An oasis is a fertile spot in a desert where there's enough water to allow plants to grow,' explained Relly when Ogi Ogi looked confused at this new word. Father Rhyme had spent the next two days resting and regaining his strength whilst Pom Pom, a kind Imagino, had brought him food and drinks. Pom Pom had grown up in Mumbai in India and she wore a traditional Indian, dress called a *sari*. It's beautiful bright-coloured silk flowed and swirled around her ankles as she moved. She'd made him the most wonderful fluffalberry juice, which he thought tasted like a cross between blackcurrant and raspberry with a twist of pineapple.

Pom Pom lived at the oasis with several other Imaginos. In days gone by a large community of Imaginos had lived happily together there but more recently many had headed further North to the coast where the cool ocean breeze in the harbour was a relief from the baking, hot sun of the desert.

After Father Rhyme had rested, he'd begun to explore the tower and learn more about its history. Pom Pom thought that the tower had been built a long time ago by an Imagino called Magen. His name was carved into the wall above the tower's front door in fancy writing, the sort with extra curls on all the letters. The tower had over fifty floors and at least a hundred rooms. Most of the rooms were empty now, but it must have been a busy place in the past. Pom Pom thought the room at the top had belonged to Magen, on account of its being filled with all sorts of ancient scrolls and spell books.

The further through the rooms they explored, the more the two Imaginos discovered that the tower was full of clever secrets and inventions to make life easier in the desert. At the very bottom of the tower was a well that sank deep down into the sand so cool drinking water could be drawn from it even on the hottest days. And at the very top of the tower was fixed a little windmill whose sails turned in the slightest breeze to power a wheel that pumped some of the water out to the gardens. Both these clever contraptions worked together so fruit and vegetables could be grown all year round and the people who lived in the castle never went hungry or thirsty.

'The tower sounds absolutely fantastic,' Relly said, his eyes bright with wonder.

'In his letter, Father Rhyme said he was heading North to find a ship. We should try and catch him up so we can help him,' Ogi Ogi said.

'That's a good idea, but it took him weeks to get there last time and he's had a huge head start. We need to find a faster way of getting there than walking,' Relly replied.

They sat for a while thinking before Relly suddenly jumped up. 'I've got it!' he cried. 'We're heading to see The Prospector, but who else do we know that lives in the mountains?'

'Small Bear?' Ogi Ogi replied.

'The Eagle,' Relly said, excitedly. 'Don't you remember, the Eagle captured me and took me to the mountains. We flew so fast that the ground became a blur at times. When he swooped and turned, we must have travelled faster than a car in Abby's world. If the Eagle took us to the Tower, then it would take maybe a day at most.'

'By jingo, that's a cracking idea!' Ogi Ogi exclaimed.

As soon as they finished packing up their things the two friends headed back to the road. The sky was clear and the morning had that crisp, Autumnal feeling. Leaves on the trees were beginning to change colour from bright and dark greens to the reds and oranges of last night's fire, but only a few of them had fallen off; it would be another couple of weeks before the weather turned colder causing the leaves to drop to the ground covering it in a crunchy carpet of swirling colour. Their journey would get much harder then, especially if it started snowing.

As they rounded a corner, they came across what looked like a giant white bumblebee flying towards them. As it flew closer they could see that it was actually a fairy Imagino. She was flying haphazardly, left to right and up and down. It didn't look like she was paying attention to what she was doing or where she was going. The two friends stopped walking and she came closer and closer. Just before she hit them, she realised they were there and stopped suddenly.

'Eeek!' she shrieked. 'What on Earth are you two doing creeping up on Imaginos like that? I could have cast a spell and turned you into a frog or anything. I am a fairy godmother you know. Or at least I was.'

'Sorry,' Ogi Ogi replied. He felt embarrassed, so turned a darker shade of green than normal. 'We didn't mean to scare you. Are you alright? You seemed to be flying all over the place.'

'Bent wing,' she replied. 'Name's Crystal. I got bashed up by the General and his cronies and it hasn't straightened out yet. I'm going to be flying in circles for weeks. If I hadn't run out of pixie dust, I'd have zapped him right between the eyes.'

With that, she landed in a heap on the floor and gave a jolly laugh. 'Ooops, I can't land very well either. I never really got the hang of it.'

'You've seen the General and his men?' Relly asked.

'I did. They roughed me up, the brutish oafs. They wanted to know if I'd seen someone. They spent ages pushing me around, but I just can't remember things so well these days, so there's not much point really. I should have stuck me wand in his belly and given it a good poke. He's a mean faced bully who needs a boil on his nose.'

'Do you know who they were searching for? Was it Father Rhyme?' Ogi Ogi asked.

'Father Time you say?' Crystal replied.

'No Rhyme, not Time. He's an old Imagino and he

talks in rhymes most of the time. We're looking for him,' Ogi Ogi said.

Crystal sat in the road pondering. She rubbed the end of her wand as she screwed her face up in concentration.

'Now you mention it, I think that's who they were after. They were pulling The Prospector's cottage apart when they stopped me. It'll take him weeks to put it back together, the poor man. They were enjoying it as well, the measly weasel-faced goons; it's an utter waste of good furniture.'

'Oh no,' Ogi Ogi gasped, 'The Prospector will be hopping mad. We'd better hurry and see if there's anything we can do to help. At least Father Rhyme hasn't been caught yet.'

'Make sure you give that stinker the General what for,' Crystal said. With that, she started to flap her wings furiously. She slowly rose off the ground, but instead of moving forward in a straight line, she began to go round and round in circles.

'It's alright,' she said. 'This is how I take off now. It's a slingshot, you see. Once I'm up to speed, I straighten out, otherwise I can't quite get enough speed to get off the ground. Wings not quite what they were. Right, that's it. Bye, boys!'

The two friends looked on in amazement as Crystal shot off diagonally, narrowly avoiding a tree before disappearing into the distance. They gathered their things and hurried along the path towards The Prospector's cottage. They were concerned about Father Rhyme and Ogi Ogi's swirling gases turned a very dark green with worry.

'I hope we're not too late to stop the General capturing Father Rhyme,' Ogi Ogi said.

'I know,' Relly replied, 'that bully needs to be stopped before he gets any closer to finding the crown.'

They both started jogging up the Northern Road. As they trotted around the next bend, they spotted a balloon way off in the distance. Its many colours looked beautifully bright against the blue sky.

'What's that?' Ogi Ogi asked, pointing into the distance.

'Gosh,' Relly replied, 'it looks like a hot air balloon. I bet that's Father Rhyme! Do you remember his child liked planes and flying? We read about them watching the planes fly over during the war and writing down which ones they'd seen. He must have got away. Quickly, we'd better hurry.'

As they started to run up the road towards The Prospector's cottage, the balloon began to sink lower in the sky. After five minutes it had dropped so low it disappeared completely. Ogi Ogi was out of breath and his gases were swirling superfast. Neither of them was used to running long distances and they were already tired.

'What do you think's happened to the balloon?' Ogi Ogi asked. 'It's nowhere to be seen.'

'I'm not sure,' said Relly, 'but it can't be good news.'

Despite trying desperately, Father Rhyme had failed to relight the oil lamp and the balloon had slowly drifted down to the ground, eventually becoming entangled in a tree. He'd seen the General and his guards as he flew over The Prospector's cottage and he knew they were chasing him. He'd finally managed to relight the lamp but it was too late; the balloon's basket was stuck on a branch of a tree and he couldn't work it free. His heart sank as the General, Lundy and several guards arrived at the base of the tree and pulled the balloon back to the ground.

'Ha ha ha,' the General cackled. 'You old fool. Did you really think you'd escape me? My power is second to none! Now it's time for you to show us exactly where you were going in this tatty balloon of yours.'

I may be trapped in the wood
But it'll do you no good
Wrong never wins
As Right never gives in

The General sneered at him. Once they'd dragged the balloon back down to the ground, the General, Lundy and two of his less idiotic guards clambered into the basket. They turned the oil lamp up to full blast to try and fill the balloon with hot air, but there were too many of them and the basket was too heavy to take off. The General started throwing things out of the basket. The bags of sand that are used to balance the balloon went first, but it stayed firmly stuck on the ground. Next he turned his attention to Father Rhyme's provisions of food and water, flinging it all to the ground and emptying the bottles of water.

If we crash in the desert
You'll be sorry, I think
To have wasted our water
So you can't have a drink

'So that's where we're going!' the General crowed triumphantly. 'We're heading across the desert! And I didn't even need to apply the thumb screws. I might anyway, just to see what sort of noise you make. Perhaps you'll squeal like a fat, hairy little piggy. The rest of you idiots need to head back to the stronghold and await our return. You must protect the mirror.'

Father Rhyme looked at the General with both pity and sorrow. As a young Imagino he might have been angry, but he'd grown wise with age. He could see straight through the General to his black heart. He didn't know whether the General knew about the crown or not, but it was clear that he knew Father Rhyme was on a mission. He'd need to do whatever he could to keep the General from finding out where he was going. His only hope was Relly and Ogi Ogi finding his note and somehow getting ahead of them.

As the last bread roll tumbled over the side of the basket, the balloon began to rise slowly into the sky and the General and Father Rhyme drifted towards the Eastern Desert. The rest of the General's guards watched as it became smaller and smaller, until it finally disappeared.

Relly and Ogi Ogi were both out of breath by the time they arrived at The Prospector's cottage. Ogi Ogi's green gases were swirling quickly and he felt like he might collapse at any minute. They both flopped on the floor and Relly fell backwards sticking his legs up in the air. There was no-one at the cottage, but there were signs that the General had beaten them too it. Most of The Prospector's furniture was broken up into pieces and scattered outside the cottage. The scene of destruction seemed eerily quiet and sad.

'Look!' Relly shouted. 'It's the balloon again.'

The balloon was taking off in the distance. It rose slowly higher and higher and then began to gather speed as it climbed up into the clouds. They watched as it shrank smaller and smaller, until it looked like a tiny bubble floating on the breeze. Far off in the distance they could see a group of guards walking back towards the cottage.

'The guards are coming,' whispered Relly. 'Quick, let's hide!'

Ogi Ogi was very worried. What if they were captured? His bottom gave a fruitful burp and he parped loudly. He used the beret to try and quickly waft it away. Relly screwed his face up at the smell and set off quickly towards The Prospector's cottage. Ogi Ogi was so frightened that he stayed rooted to the ground, so Relly came back, despite the smell, grabbed him by the hand and dragged him out of sight. Once they were inside the cottage, Relly put his fingers to his lips to show they needed to be extra quiet.

The guards arrived and began gathering their things. They looked miserable and one of them started jumping up and down on the broken furniture that lay littered around the cottage.

'Oi, what's that stink?' one of them said, screwing up his face in a disgusted manner.

'It's probably you. He who smelt it dealt it,' another accused.

'It ain't me, you cheeky monkey,' the first guard replied. 'I bet it's you, you're always eating too much and making a wiffy smell. I won't be marching behind you.'

The two guards began to push each other around, which developed into a proper scuffle, resulting in them both rolling around on the floor.

'Hey! Stop that right now,' a third guard said. 'Get up and pack your things. You heard the General, we need to get back and protect the mirror. If we don't get to the Southern Forest soon, one of those do-gooding Imaginos might stick their nose in. If we lose the mirror we're going to be in big trouble when he gets back!'

Relly and Ogi Ogi looked at each other in surprise. Before they could say anything, they began to have that falling feeling. They felt like they'd gone a tiny bit dizzy and were just about to fall in on themselves. The world of Imago slowly began to fade.

CHAPTER ELEVEN

SCHOOL TRIP

A bby was super excited: today was the school trip to London! Her mum had woken her up extra early to make sure they arrived at the playground in time. It was five o'clock in the morning when her mum had come into her bedroom and pulled the covers back. Outside it was still completely dark and it felt more like Winter than Autumn.

Jane and Abby had managed to find seats next to each other on the coach. They watched as the dimly lit countryside flashed past their window. They were both tired and the time flew by as they drew closer to the city. The coach stopped at a train station with a 'Park And Ride' on the edge of London. This meant they could leave the coach behind and catch a train to the centre of the Capital. Everything seemed so big and busy in London and the train was full of what Mrs Fowler referred to as 'commuters'.

'I can't see any computers on the train,' Stephen Wolvesgrove said.

'No, the train's full of commuters,' Mrs Fowler said.

'What's a commuter, Miss?' Stephen Wolvesgrove asked.

'A person who doesn't live in the same town as they work so they have to get up very early every day and then travel a long way to work. Some people have to spend an hour or more travelling before they get to work,' Mrs Fowler replied. 'And they don't arrive home until late at night.'

'That doesn't sound like fun,' Stephen replied.

The train pulled into Euston Station where they walked along a series of brightly-lit passages and travelled on the longest escalators they'd ever seen to catch an underground train known as 'the tube' to the museum. None of the children had been on the tube before and it was quite an adventure. The escalators were packed with people and they had to stand on the right so all the busy people could rush past on the left. Once they reached the platform, Mrs Fowler rounded them up into a group close enough so they could all hear her.

'Now we must stay together,' she said. 'If anyone gets lost, they must find a police officer and ask for help. I've given you all a card which has my phone number and the school's number on. When the next train arrives, half of you will get on the train with me and the other half with Miss Symnett. That's sixteen children with me and fifteen with Miss Symnett.'

The train pulled in to the station and they were swept aboard with a wave of passengers. There was even less space on the tube than the train. People were squashed in like sardines. The doors closed and a tinny sounding message came from the speakers telling people to 'Mind the doors, please.' The tube whizzed into the tunnel and suddenly it was black like the very darkest night outside, turning the windows into mirrors. Jane guessed it was called 'the tube' because the trains travelled along tunnels like a series of underground tubes.

'Right, children, this is the Northern Line and we are heading south to the museum. Just two stops and then we need to get off at Goodge Street and walk the last part,' Mrs Fowler said.

'We're g-g-g-going South and North, Miss?' Arthur Moss asked.

Mrs Fowler smiled kindly, 'The tube lines all have different names, Arthur. This one's called the Northern Line, but at the moment we're actually travelling South. It's a bit confusing but the maps on the walls show you all the different lines and stations. Each one has a colour and the one we're on now is black.'

Jane and Abby smiled when they heard Mrs Fowler speak so kindly and patiently to Arthur. Recently he'd been giving Arthur extra help with his stammer and it was now almost gone.

The tube pulled into Goodge Street and the children were bundled out of the carriage. After a quick head count, Mrs Fowler led them to the escalators and they burst out from the station into the busy city above. The pavements were full of more people than they had ever seen before and the two girls agreed that London was the busiest place they had ever been. It was like they were ants in a great big colony. They arrived at the wide square outside the British Museum and Mrs Fowler quickly counted them again. The museum had a fabulous grand entrance with dozens of pillars and large thick wooden doors. Once you went inside there was a huge white interior rotunda underneath a massive glass ceiling. It was like the inside was outside.

'We are here to see a remarkable new exhibition about Egypt's two lost cities,' Mrs Fowler announced, her eyes sparkling with excitement and her voice bubbling with enthusiasm. 'They were lost under the Mediterranean Ocean for over a thousand years and only recently found. *Thonis-Heracleion* was one of Egypt's most wealthy cities and *Canopus* was considered a very important city where they prayed to their gods.'

'I bet there's treasure,' gasped Tom Clark.

'There will be all sorts of artefacts and treasures,' Mrs Folwer replied. 'But we must not touch anything on display unless we are told that we can do so by a member of staff. Now come along children, we are due to see the opening.'

The children made their way into the museum, chattering excitedly. Inside the big building the air was refreshingly cool and there were lots of rooms filled with all sorts of things from different eras of history. It was like an Aladdin's cave. They arrived at the entrance to the museum's Egyptian section to find a large queue of people and several other classes from different schools all waiting. A long, red ribbon stretched across the entrance to stop anyone entering the new exhibition and lots of journalists and photographers gently pushed and shoved each other, each trying to shuffle into the best position to capture the grand opening ceremony.

The museum's manager stood up and addressed the crowd. 'I'm very pleased to welcome you to this fabulous new exhibition. We're very lucky to have an expert on Egyptian artefacts here to open it for us, the right honourable Henry Harris-Smyth, Member of Parliament for Glanthorm.'

Abby and Jane gasped as Henry pushed his way to the front. The manager gave him the scissors, which looked tiny in Henry's podgy hands. He was just about to cut the ribbon when he whipped out a handkerchief and sneezed. The girls looked at each other as he blew his nose.

'Ueewwww, horrible toad bogies,' Jane whispered.

'I have great pleasure in opening this exhibition today,' Henry said in his most pompous voice. 'This discovery is an extremely important find. It tells us much about how the Egyptians lived and prayed. I declare the exhibition open.'

The scissors sliced through the tape and the crowd applauded. The doors were opened and the manager, Henry The Toad, the photographers and journalists turned and began jostling with each other to enter the exhibition. Henry sneakily put his dirty handkerchief into the handbag of the manager in front of him. She didn't notice as he dropped it in there. It must have been filthy because he was holding it with only two fingers to avoid touching the slimy material.

'Yuk, did you see that?' Jane said.

'What?' asked Abby.

'The Toad put his yucky hanky into that lady's bag. After she turned round to go into the museum he just dropped it in. What a slimy beast!'

The doors opened and the loathsome MP barged his way into the exhibition. He smiled and waved as he passed the photographers. After a long wait, the crowd of school children made its way slowly into the museum's Egyptian area. The entrance hall was huge and made mostly of pale, cream marble and dark wooden handrails and beams. A huge banner hung down from a grand staircase with the words 'Thonis-Heracleion' in historical lettering painted on it. The children followed Mrs Fowler as she led them into the exhibition.

'I bet Relly and Ogi Ogi would love to see all these treasures,' Jane said.

'Oh, you're right,' Abby said. 'They can visit and pretend to be ancient Egyptian pharaohs.'

'Or their cats,' Jane replied. 'Ancient Egyptians used to worship cats and thought they were holy.'

'Let's imagine Relly and Ogi Ogi here, Jane. It's a shame for them to miss all this,' suggested Abby. Jane readily agreed and all at once the two imaginary friends found themselves with the two girls at an exhibition of ancient Egyptian artefacts.

They all entered the exhibition and began exploring the ancient items together. The first room was filled with huge stone heads. Abby read a notice on the wall which explained they were carvings of the queens who had lived at that time. When the land had been flooded, mud from the sea bed had protected them and now they looked almost like they'd been carved just yesterday. Relly and Ogi Ogi were standing on top of the stone heads and the girls imagined them dancing to some ancient music. They were performing an Egyptian dance that involved bobbing their heads while sticking one arm behind them and one arm in front. They began to giggle as they teetered around the top of the massive stone statues. Relly began jumping from stone to stone, while Ogi Ogi sat down and pretended to be a pharaoh.

The next room of the exhibition was set up like a royal throne room and the lights were dimmed to protect some of the most fragile artefacts. A large stone throne stood in the centre of the room with a sarcophagus either side of it. The friends learned that a sarcophagus is the special box that the Egyptians used to bury their kings and queens. They decorated them with bright colours and gold and inside are the mummified remains of the royal family. There was even a special little sarcophagus for their favourite cat.

'Blimey, imagine a mummified cat,' said Jane.

'Our cat Sparky is always chasing his tail,' laughed Abby. 'I expect the mummified cat would chase its bandages round and round!'

Relly was sitting on the throne pretending to be a mummified cat, while Ogi Ogi was pretending to walk around the throne like a zombie with his arms held out in front of him. Each time Ogi Ogi passed him, Relly pretended to bat him with a paw while meowing loudly. The two girls were giggling, causing the guide to cough and look at them sternly. They stopped laughing and their two imaginary friends sat down regally on the throne, pretending to be the king and queen.

'The Pharaohs and the royal family ate meat, fruit, vegetables, and honey-sweetened cakes with fine wines. The poor had a much more boring diet of bread, fish, beans, onions and garlic, washed down with a soupy beer,' the guide said.

'Euw yuk,' Abby whispered. 'Soupy beer sounds awful.'

'How do you think the cats got in and out of the pyramids?' Jane asked quietly.

Before Abby could reply, the two girls noticed The Toad Henry sneaking behind the guide to the edge of the throne. He was shuffling slowly and had a really shifty look on his face. Whilst everyone else was looking at the guide, he positioned himself next to a table containing several stone slabs, books and scrolls. Suddenly there was a commotion as the guide stumbled and fell, knocking several children over as he tried to steady himself. The guide fell against the throne and a sarcophagus started wobbling slowly from side to side. As the guide knocked over a security barrier the screech of an alarm filled the air Relly and Ogi Ogi jumped up off the throne and stood on top of the other sarcophagus.

'Did you see him?' Jane gasped.

'Who?' Abby replied.

'The big grotty toad,' Jane replied. 'He's taken something. I saw him push the guide and then quickly grab something from the table next to the throne. He's stolen something from the exhibition. Come on, let's have a look and find out what he is up to.'

Once the guide had steadied himself, brushed himself off and settled everyone down, he resumed his talk and led the children through to the next room. The two girls hung back and then went over to the table next to the throne. It contained several stone slabs covered in Egyptian hieroglyphics and a note book which had belonged to the adventurer who discovered the lost city. Abby imagined Relly dressed as Sherlock Homes peering through a magnifying glass to try and spot any clues.

'I think there's a stone slab missing,' Abby said. 'Can you see, there's a space there, where one should be?'

'You're right, there's a big space and that notebook looks different as well. I think he's stolen the slab and replaced the notebook with a new one so that no-one realises' Jane replied. 'Come on, let's catch-up with everyone and see what he's up to now.'

By the time they caught up with the tour, Mrs Fowler had noticed the girls were missing and had a worried frown on her face, which quickly vanished when she saw the girls.

'Girls, good heavens where ever have you been?' Mrs Fowler asked.

'Sorry, Miss,' Abby said. 'We went to the toilet, I couldn't wait any longer.'

'Franck Goddio, the man who discovered the hidden city, will be giving a talk in a minute,' Mrs Fowler said. 'Do hurry up because I'm sure it will be interesting.'

Mrs Fowler hurried them along and they shuffled towards the front of the crowd. A neat looking man with a friendly smile was standing at the front with a microphone. The Toad stood behind him grinning from ear to ear for the television cameras and journalists, his podgy red face and round nose bobbing from side to side like a crazy clown.

'Underwater archaeology is a new science,' Franck explained. 'Whilst searching the seabed for an eighteenth Century French warship, we discovered the legendary city of Heracleion. The city was home to the last pharaoh of Ancient Egypt, Cleopatra VII Philopator, known to history as Cleopatra. We think her empire was destroyed by an earthquake and tidal waves, but the sand of the sea preserved all of these wonderful artefacts for us to see.'

Abby suddenly got a terrible stinky waft up her nose. It smelled like mouldy cabbages mixed with baked beans. She elbowed Jane in the ribs and then pointed at her, holding her nose and raising her eyebrows in a questioning way. Jane looked shocked and shook her head.

'Ewwwww!' Abby whispered. 'Is that Ogi Ogi letting off wind again?'

'Not this time,' Jane replied with a cheeky smile. 'I think it's someone on the stage. That poor explorer must be getting gassed. I bet it's Henry Harris-Smyth MP for Stinkseville Pongytown.'

'Look there, in his pocket,' Abby said quietly. She pointed it out to Jane. 'Can you see there's a stone slab just peeking out?'

'He's definitely stolen it,' Jane said. 'We'd better tell someone before he gets away with it.'

Relly and Ogi Ogi had their fingers over their noses and were trying to waft the smell away. Relly had started hopping from one foot to the other and was pointing at the Egyptian slab in The Toad's pocket.

The speech ended and the school children were ushered towards the exit. Jane and Abby tried to get Mrs Folwer's attention, but she was too busy trying to count them count whilst also being pushed out of the room by the other children from the other schools. The girls could see The Toad talking to the explorer and Abby could have sworn he winked at her. Arthur Moss was missing, so the whole class had to wait in the entrance hall whilst the teaching assistant, Mrs Morgan, searched for him. Mrs Fowler looked very worried and the girls could tell that she was distracted and not listening to them as they tried to tell her about the missing notebook and stone slab.

After what seemed like forever, Mrs Morgan appeared with a tearful Arthur Moss. He'd run off when the alarm went off and got lost. The teachers did the head count again and everyone was finally there. They were just about to leave when Henry Harris-Smyth walked towards them with a great big grin on his face. Just before he walked past the class, he stopped and turned to Mrs Fowler.

'Ah madam,' he said. 'Delighted to meet you again. Good to see our school's getting out and seeing a bit of culture.'

'Hello,' she replied. 'Yes, it's been a wonderful visit and I'm sure the children have learned a lot about Egyptian history.'

He turned and began to walk towards the exit, then stopped as he reached Abby and Jane.

'Hope you enjoyed the exhibition, girls,' he said in his oily voice, then he leaned in so that they could feel his horrible breath on their faces as he whispered. 'There were lots of precious artefacts to look at. I will be very much looking forward to visiting Imago myself one day.' Laughing to himself, he waddled away, patting his pocket, as he left the museum as fast as his podgy legs could carry him.

Mrs Fowler rounded up the children and herded them out of the museum and along the busy streets to the tube station. Everyone was accounted for and apart from the incident with Arthur, the trip had been a great success. She breathed a relieved sigh as the train set off and whooshed into the tunnel. Smiling to herself as she thought of her favourite, comfortable armchair and fluffy slippers waiting for her at home. She didn't notice Abby and Jane making their wobbly way along the carriage until they were standing right next to her and Jane spoke, 'Miss, I think something's been stolen from the exhibition.'

'Miss, it was that horrible MP,' added Abby.

'Oh don't be silly, girls,' Mrs Fowler replied a little impatiently. 'You do have such active imaginations, I think you need to focus that on our *big write* tomorrow. If there'd been a theft, the alarm would have gone off!'

'But it did go off,' Jane said.

'Oh yes, but that was when the guide fell over and knocked the barrier. No need to worry girls, it was just an accident,' Mrs Fowler said, keen to return to her daydream of comfy slippers and the exciting book she was part-way through reading.

The girls were frustrated that Mrs Fowler wasn't taking them seriously. She was their teacher and also their friend and if she didn't believe them, who would? Jane turned to

Abby, 'What did that beastly oaf mean when he said he'd be "visiting Imago"?'

'I don't know but he's definitely up to something and we need to tell someone. Mrs Fowler was so worried about Arthur it's no wonder she wouldn't listen to us. We need to find someone who will believe us and help us find out what The Toad is up to.'

As the girls swayed on the rumbling underground train, a frustrated Relly and Ogi Ogi faded back into Imago. They wanted to find out what had happened to the stolen exhibits and what Henry Harris-Smyth was up to. But there was little they could do until the girls imagined them back into their world again.

CHAPTER TWELVE

OLD FRIENDS

Upon their return to Imago from the museum, Relly and Ogi Ogi were greeted by a bright Autumn sun. Relly found himself sitting upon the roof of The Prospector's cottage and Ogi Ogi appeared inside next to the remains of the broken table. Relly threw himself down onto the roof and tried to make himself as small as possible. He had no idea where the General's guards were, but it wouldn't be hard for them to see him. He tried to look around but he could only see his side of the roof.

'Psssssssst, Ogi Ogi,' Relly hissed under his breath.

'Hey, what's that?' shouted Ogi Ogi in response.

'Shhhhhhhhhhhhhhh,' Relly hissed.

'That awful beret: it's gone,' Ogi Ogi said dancing a little jig. 'I thought I'd never be rid of it.'

'Never mind about that,' Relly said. 'What about the guards, do you think they've gone?'

'Oooops,' Ogi Ogi replied, 'let me have a look.'

Ogi Ogi moved quickly from window to window searching the horizon for the General's troops.

'I can't see anything. I've looked out of all the windows and it looks like they've gone. Where are you? I'm hungry,' Ogi Ogi said.

'You're always hungry! I'm up on the roof,' Relly said. 'I didn't want to stand up in case they saw me. Let me have a look.'

Relly stood up and started to look around. Imago looked beautiful. The sunshine on his back kept him warm despite the slight chill of the wind. He looked in each direction until eventually he saw the guards in the distance. They were marching South on the road to Creatown. Even from a distance they looked a scruffy, disorganised bunch of twits. He shuffled down the roof on his bottom and slid down the drainpipe. It was slippier than he expected and he ended up shooting down the pipe and tumbling out onto the floor.

'They've gone,' Relly announced.

After Ogi Ogi had recovered from a fit of giggles, he sat down on the cottage porch and rubbed his head thoughtfully. 'What do you think we should do next?' he asked.

'Catch those guards and open up a can of whoop-ass on those darn stoopid soldiers,' came the loud response from a very dusty looking Imagino.

'The Prospector!' Relly and Ogi Ogi both cried.

'The very same,' The Prospector replied. 'When I get my hands on those varmints, why I will roast their toes on my camp fire. I'd make them put every bit of furniture back together if they weren't so stoopid. They'd end up making a boat from a chair. The boneheaded baboons wouldn't know their behind from their elbow.'

Relly and Ogi Ogi dashed over and gave him a great big hug.

'You will never guess what just happened,' Relly said quickly. 'There was a balloon and we think Father Rhyme was in it. He's crossing the desert.'

'Whoa! Hang on a cotton-pickin' minute there. Slow your horses down,' The Prospector replied. 'We'd better head up into the mountains in case those varmints come back again. I saw that there balloon come down and I tried to reach it to help the pilot, but I was too slow.'

He led them to the hidden tunnel at the base of the mountains. At first it looked like a narrow gap in the rocks but once they squeezed through they found themselves at the entrance to the mines. The Prospector lit the oil lamp and led them further underground into the mountains. The two friends weren't scared because they'd been under the mountains before when they'd first met The Prospector, and they trusted him.

It wasn't long before they reached the underground store where he kept his tools. It was a large cavern filled with piles of wooden crates and a small stove with a chimney running up into the rock above. Ogi Ogi's tummy rumbled as he remembered the last time they'd stopped here and been offered some delicious, spicy bean stew. But there was no stew this time and they quickly ducked into the left hand tunnel and started zigzagging upwards towards The Propsector's home. It was a long, steep climb and the two friends were soon out of breath and dripping with sweat. After what seemed like hours, they reached a wooden hatch above them. The Prospector knocked on it four times. He used a pattern of three quiet and one loud knock.

'Knock, knock, knock...KNOCK!'

They heard a bolt slide open and a key turn before the hatch opened and light flooded out. Looking down at the three of them was the smiling face of Small Bear. They'd met him in Mushroontan on their last adventure. He'd always wanted to see the mines and hunt for gems in the mountains, so he'd joined them on their quest. He proved himself to be a fearless companion. After they'd managed to speak to Abby and Jane through their dreams and tell them about the wicked Princess Marjorie, he'd stayed behind in the mountains with The Prospector to hunt for diamonds and gold.

'Relly! Ogi Ogi!' Small Bear cried.

They quickly climbed into The Prospector's mountain home and gave the Small Bear a huge hug.

'It's so good to see you,' Relly said. 'How have you been? Did you find any treasure?'

'We found a heap of silver last month,' Small Bear replied. 'We were deep under Fygnord Peak to the Western side of the mountains when we hit a seam of silver that glittered like the sun. We've got four buckets-worth waiting to be cleaned up and turned into bars. But what about you two? What's been happening? We don't hear much news here.'

The Prospector brewed some tea and fetched some ginger biscuits whilst Relly and Ogi Ogi began to tell them what had happened since the Eagle had flown them home. Once they'd returned to the castle, the Princess had seen the error of her ways. She ordered the guards to arrest the General but some of them were still loyal to him. The General fled the castle, but since then he'd been seen all over Imago making a nuisance of himself. They'd wanted to see how you he was and find out if Father Rhyme had returned home, so they went to his shop to look for him.

'And that's when we discovered this,' Relly said, pulling Father Rhyme's journal out of his bag.

'It's his journal: it's fascinating!' Ogi Ogi said. 'It's a diary of his life and it's full of maps of Imago, riddles and poems. He'd hidden it for us to find because he knew that the General would try and catch him. We think he's come North to try and find a magic crown. We need to find him and help him. If the General gets hold of it, who knows what wickedness he will get up to.'

'Well, you two had better tell us everything you know about this 'ere journal then,' said The Prospector, making himself comfortable.

Relly and Ogi Ogi began by showing them the letter Father Rhyme had left telling them to look for the book. Next they read through the sections on the Needle Tower and then finally the rhyme which described the three objects of power.

'Blimey,' said Small Bear. 'That tiny needle pointing up into the sky in the desert is a tower and it's got Imaginos in it. Wow, there's a sea port as well. I wonder if there are pirates and treasure! What does the journal say about the sea? Did Father Rhyme sail on the Endless Ocean?'

They began to search through the book until they found the section about his journey to the seaport. After several months at the Needle Tower with Pom Pom and her friends, he'd decided to explore the ocean.

'Hang on...what's this bit?' said Small Bear.

I had finally realised just how powerful Magen had been. In his tower he'd created three tremendous objects of power. His spell books described the ability to make a link between Imago and the world of our children. But in the wrong hands they could be used to control worlds and even give people everlasting life. For that reason he'd hidden all of the objects apart

from one. He'd made a beautiful crown but its power
was so great that he became intoxicated by it. It cast a
spell over him. He'd sat and worn it each day growing
older and older in his room at the top of the tower.
I knew that I had to hide the crown and make sure
it was never found again. So I locked his tower and
headed towards the cove to find a ship.

'He must have taken it across the sea,' squealed Small Bear with excitement. 'Can I come? Pleeeeasssee! Oh I want to see the sea and travel on a ship.'

Small Bear began hopping from foot to foot with excitement whilst Ogi Ogi went from light green to dark green and started to frown, a sure sign that he was deep in thought.

'I hope you don't get sea sick,' Relly said. 'Let's see if there are more clues in the journal.

They searched the huge journal until they found the sections describing the sea journey. Father Rhyme described his voyage in detail. Once he'd found a ship, he'd spent two weeks at sea sailing further and further north until they'd arrived at three uninhabited islands.

'He's written a rhyme to describe where he left it,' Ogi Ogi said:

Across the waves you must travel
If this riddle you hope to unravel
First, look to the stars up high
Shining brightly in the sky
Follow them to the edge of the world
Where the green sea boils and huge waves swirl
There three islands you will find:

Pick the right one and make up your mind
With the peak to your left, head for the centre
Look for the cave that you need to enter
Don't be afraid of the teeth overhead
Even though they may fill you with dread
Once land is made, follow the light;
You will need to reach quite a height
Once at the top with the sun on your back
Take ten paces forward onto the track
Stop just here and turn to your right
Wiggle through the rocks, ever so tight
Look for the worms to find your prize
Place it on your head and a king will arise

'So, the crown is on the middle island!' Ogi Ogi said.

'I don't think we will know which one until we get there. The rhyme said we need to head for the centre peak and we'd need to see them to know which is which,' Relly said. 'We need to hurry because the General is ahead of us and the balloon will zoom along at super speed.'

'You folks need to skedaddle, otherwise you ain't ever gonna beat that varmint,' The Prospector replied.

'We hoped that the Eagle would fly us to the tower because it would be much quicker than walking. Do you think he will help us?' Relly asked.

'That half-witted bird's crazier than ever,' The Prospector replied. 'He's either sitting on that egg he found or off looking for things to make his nest bigger. He stops by most days to say howdie, so I dare say you can ask him.'

'There's no time to lose,' Relly said. 'I really think we should get going as soon as possible. The General could have reached the tower already.'

'Whoa there partner! Hold your horses!' The Prospector said. 'Before you dash off head first into the desert, you'd better find out what you're up against. All sorts of dangers could be waiting for you and I dare say this journal of Father Rhyme's has a few more secrets to tell.'

'But we don't have time,' Relly pleaded. 'We've got to catch them as soon as possible to make sure we get to the crown first.'

'Calm down young 'un' he replied. 'Let me shimmy on up to the Eagle's nest and see if the feathered fuss pot is there. I'm quicker than you and I can be there and back in no time. Meanwhile, you three look through the journal to see if you can find out any more about the tower or the crown.'

The Prospector lifted up the hatch to the mountain top room and quickly disappeared into his maze of tunnels. Meanwhile the three friends looked through the journal for more clues. They searched the pages until they found a long passage describing the wizard Magen's tower:

Pom Pom took me up to the top of the tower. The spiral staircase ran along the outside wall of the tower. Each floor had a large circular room on it which Imaginos either lived or worked in. The rooms at the bottom were used for jobs like cooking and cleaning. Next came the dining and living areas and finally the bedrooms. The staircase seemed to keep turning around and around forever like an enormous cork screw. By the time I'd passed the first ten doors, I felt like I'd been spinning on a roundabout too long. I couldn't hold on any more and stars started flashing before my eyes. Thankfully, we stopped in a large bedroom, which must have once been inhabited by an Imagino who liked very bright costumes. All sorts of wonderful outfits hung from wardrobes and bedposts. There was even a fine court jester's costume with a hat that had jingly bells on it.

After I'd rested, Pom Pom led me up the dimly-lit stairs once more. One, two, three, the doors slowly passed as we climbed higher and higher...ten, eleven, twelve...until finally we reached the fiftieth door at the very top of the stairs. Pom Pom took a key from a silver chain around her neck, said the secret words, and the door slowly creaked open. Light flooded out and almost blinded me. Once my eyes had adjusted, I could see that the room was crammed full of stuff. There were piles of scrolls, a huge desk, models of mechanical devices, maps pinned to the wall, several cauldrons and what looked like a giant chemistry set; and in the far corner, a metal staircase leading to a rooftop observatory. In the observatory stood a telescope pointing up towards a hatch, which could be opened to reveal the beautiful night sky.

And so began the next part of my adventure. I spent the following few months reading scrolls, studying maps and best of all looking at the moon and stars through the telescope. Magen had created detailed maps of the stars in the night sky. He'd labelled the constellations (they are the groups of stars) and written their names next to them. Where they were the same as our children's world, he'd made a note. He was particularly interested in a group of stars called Ursa Major, which is also known as the Great Bear or the Plough. He'd built a model of them which he'd hung from the ceiling.

Many of the scrolls compared Imago with the world of our children, Earth. He had tried, on a number of occasions, to speak with his child who no longer played with him. The scrolls documented his attempts and the different inventions he'd tried until he finally succeeded. He'd waited until the moon and the stars were aligned and then cast powerful spells to make a magic mirror, which he'd used to speak to his child at last.

'My goodness,' Ogi Ogi said. 'You don't think that the wicked General has the same mirror do you?'

'I do,' Relly replied nervously. 'I bet he was speaking to his grown up child and I've no doubt they are an absolute beast as well. I bet they're rotten to the core.'

The hatch flew open and The Prospector burst back in. 'Darn it! That blasted buzzard brain is off somewhere. I've left him a note to tell him to come see us straight away. What have you found then, eh?'

'The wizard who lived in the tower made a magic mirror,' Small Bear said, fidgeting excitedly. 'He used it to speak to his child. Can you imagine? It's amazing!'

'Ooooooooeeeeee! Ain't that a fine dandy thing,' said The Prospector, as he scratched his beard. 'We'd better grab some tucker and hunker down for the night. We can read more of that there book while we wait for that blasted bird to show-up.'

As the sun started to set, the four friends settled down for the night. Whilst they were eating, they swapped stories from the last few months. Small Bear had explored most of the mines and had been helping The Prospector with the eastern most tunnel, where they'd discovered a rich vein of silver. Before bed, they gathered around Father Rhyme's journal and began searching for clues to the crown's secrets.

CHAPTER THIRTEEN

CRASH LANDING

Father Rhyme cursed his bad luck. If the lamp hadn't gone out he wouldn't have landed and the General and his stinking guards wouldn't have captured him. Now he was crammed into the basket with the General and three of his guards. One of them smelled like mouldy, gone-off socks that had been dipped in yogurt and left to go crispy in the sun. To make matters worse, the General's belly took up too much room and Father Rhyme felt like he was going to be pushed over the side any minute.

'So we're off across the desert then are we, you ancient fool?' the General asked.

'Your nasty tricks won't get you far, even if we float up to the stars,' Father Rhyme replied.

The General laughed and slapped one of his guards on the back. Father Rhyme gazed out across the approaching desert. He wasn't going to let this oaf spoil his balloon ride. He'd imagined flying across Imago for years and now he was finally realising his dream.

Once they were level with the first snow on the mountains, the wind picked up and they started to gather speed. Father Rhyme decided to turn the flame down to stop them going too high. He knew that the higher he flew the colder it would be; eventually the air would become so thin that he would find it difficult to breathe. He reached out to the knob on the lamp and the General rapped Father Rhyme's knuckles with his fist.

'No you don't, you old goat. You leave the lamp alone, we're doing just fine as we are,' the General barked.

'Well if you want to go so high you freeze, you can do as you please,' Father Rhyme replied.

They climbed higher and higher as the balloon gained more speed. The temperature started to drop and they could soon see their breath in front of their faces. Father Rhyme was starting to feel a little dizzy. He was too old for the thin air and the cold.

'Sir?' Lundy chipped in. 'Had we better lose a little bit of height now? It's getting a bit chilly and we haven't got our thick uniforms on.'

'Nonsense, we're zipping along like a jet engine. At this rate we will cross the desert before sunset,' the General said.

'But what if we catch a cold Sir? That would slow us down, or worse. If the oil in the lamp freezes, it might stop burning? We'd drop out of the sky like a dead duck,' Lundy said.

'Hmmm, alright. Come on then Mr Rhyme-all-the-time, turn it down a bit and take us back to a safe level, but if you try and land the balloon I will take your fingers and bend them so far back you will think they were put on backwards,' the General said.

Father Rhyme dutifully turned the lamp down and they dropped several hundred metres. Once they'd reached a safe level, he steadied the balloon. He looked down as the desert flew past. You might think all that sand would be a boring sight, but it was a wonderful view. The colours changed from yellow to orange as the sand dunes went up and down. Sometimes huge red rocks rose out of the desert, casting long black shadows. As the hours ticked by, the Needle Tower started to get closer and Father Rhyme wondered how fast they were going. It had taken him at least a week to travel this far when he'd walked there before.

'What's that tower in the distance then?' the General asked.

'You will see in not so long, but it won't help you do more wrong,' Father Rhyme replied.

'I bet that's where you were headed, you decrepit old bumbler,' the General growled.

Another couple of hours passed and the sun had started to go down. They could see the tower clearly and lights in the windows showed that someone was home. Father Rhyme knew they'd need to start bringing the balloon down soon or they'd shoot straight past. But he waited until as late as possible so they'd end up having to walk back to the tower. He hoped that whoever lived there now would see them coming and hide from the General and his idiot guards.

'We're going to miss it, you fool,' the General cried. 'Bring us down or I will throw you over the side. Grab his ankles, boys!'

Father Rhyme quickly adjusted the lamp and they began to head down towards the desert. As they drifted downwards, the wind dropped and they began to slow, but they were still going too fast and the tower was soon upon them. The tower was surrounded by an oasis, bursting with wonderful trees, plants and birds. They could see a small well in the centre. The balloon whizzed past the tower and the oasis before dropping to within a few metres of the ground. They needed to slow down or they'd hit the ground at high speed. Father Rhyme pushed the soldiers out of the way and grabbed a couple of heavy sand bags with rope tied onto them. He was about to throw them out, when the General shouted for him to stop.

'These will help us stop, you stupid clot,' Father Rhyme cried out to the General.

The bags tumbled over the side and dug into the sand dunes below, shaking the balloon so that Father Rhyme nearly fell over the side. He grabbed hold of the basket and quickly turned the lamp off. Despite the balloon slowing down, they still hit the ground hard and all went flying out of the basket in different directions. Father Rhyme landed on his bottom with a thump. It didn't feel like he'd hurt himself too badly so he pulled himself up. His legs ached, more from age than the crash landing, but he knew he had to try and get to the tower before the General and warn the Imaginos who lived there. He scrambled up and started to walk through the sand towards the tower. He could hear the General arguing with Lundy behind him, which spurred him on to get there first. Walking through deep sand is like wading through water and Father Rhyme felt his feet sinking into the sand with each step. It was hard to pick his feet up but he trudged onwards until at last, he slid down the final dune and found himself in the oasis that surrounded the tower. As he drew closer to the tower, he could hear the guards shouting behind him and he knew they'd catch him before he reached it. Then he saw an Imagino in front of him. It was a dog, a scruffy looking dog.

'Hello,' it said. 'My names Scraffles. Are you alright?

'Does Pom Pom still live here?' he asked. He was so out of breath that he was panting like a dog himself.

'Yes she does,' Scraffles said. 'Why, do you know her?'

Give her a message from old Father Rhyme
She must leave now while there is still time
An Imagino known as the General is here
With his wicked guards whom you should fear
He's trying to find the wizard's crown
He'll use it to bring Imago down

'What do you mean?' Scraffles asked.

'Please go and warn them and I will try to slow them down,' he pleaded.

Scraffles could see how desperate Father Rhyme was so he ran back to the tower to warn the others. Father Rhyme could hear the guards searching for him. He'd thought about trying to run and hide, but he knew he'd be too slow, so he decided to act like he'd hurt himself. He lay down on the floor and started to groan quietly.

'Ooooooooeerrrrrrrr,' he moaned.

After another five minutes or so, the General and his guards found Father Rhyme lying down underneath a large palm tree.

'What's wrong with him?' barked the General.

'Whhhheeerrrreee am I?' Father Rhyme whispered.

'I think the old boy's hurt himself,' Lundy said. 'We'd better not move him in case he's broken something.'

'We haven't got time for this nonsense,' the General said grumpily. 'Throw some water on the old codger, that will soon wake him up.'

One of the guards took his water bottle out of his bag and poured it onto Father Rhyme's head. Rather than react or jump straight up, he continued to moan and groan.

'My legs, my legs,' he muttered. 'What on Imago is going on? Where am I?'

'You're at the tower in the desert,' Lundy said cheerfully. 'You can't lie around here, it's getting dark. You need to get up, come on!'

'What tower? I'm afraid my legs have no power. I can't possibly move,' Father Rhyme replied.

'Right you lot, grab two large sticks and make a stretcher,' the General ordered. 'We will carry the old fool if he refuses to move. Come on, we haven't got all day. It's going to be dark soon. Who knows what snakes and scorpions live in this place.'

The two guards made a stretcher and then picked up Father Rhyme and carried him to the tower. They dropped him on the ground outside the door. Father Rhyme carefully looked out of the corner of his eye to see if the tower was empty. The lights in the windows had gone out, but he wouldn't know if they'd left until they went inside themselves.

The General knocked on the large wooden doors. When there was no answer, he tried the heavy brass handle. The doors were unlocked and they made a large clonk as he lifted the latch. Creeeeaaaaakkkkkkkkk went the doors as they slowly swung open. The tower looked deserted; it was dark and completely silent. The guards' boots made a heavy thumping noise as they walked into the centre of the entrance hall.

'Search the place from top to bottom!' the General barked at the guards before turning to Father Rhyme. 'Right, you slippery old twister. You'd better stop pretending to be brain dead and start talking. I want to know where you're going and what you are looking for.

I know you helped those two meddlesome Imaginos Relly and Ogi Ogi. They must have had a magic object of some kind to be able to speak to their children. So what was it?'

Father Rhyme could hear the guards crashing around the tower. He didn't want it to be smashed up because of him but if he didn't say anything the general would order them to tear the place apart. What's more, he wanted them to leave the tower as quickly as possible so the Imaginos that lived there could return home. He sat there deep in thought. Perhaps he should tell the General something.

'Well, I know some of it, you buffoon,' the General said. He held up a battered old notebook. 'I found that old mine rat's "Busyness log". It contains a description of a milky looking stone that allowed him to speak to his grown-up child in his dreams. I bet that's what those two annoying Imaginos used, isn't it? Is that what you're looking for now?'

Oh dear, oh dear, thought Father Rhyme, he's found out about the dream stone. Another loud smashing sound made him jump. It sounded like something made of glass. The General stormed up to him and shook him by both arms.

'You'd better start talking or we will smash the whole place up, bit by bit,' the General said.

'It's not the stone I'm looking for. To the North I head for a sandy shore,' Father Rhyme said.

'North, north, what's north of here?' the General said.

'Why, the sea of course,' Father Rhyme replied.

'The ocean is endless you fool, everyone knows that,' the General replied.

'Have they sailed the ocean? Have they seen its beautiful waves in motion?' Father Rhyme asked.

'I know there's another magic object in Imago and I want it. I can tell you're looking for it and if you're heading across the ocean, then that's where we will go. You can tell me more about it along the way or you will find the journey a very unpleasant one indeed,' the General threatened.

It took the guards several hours to search the tower. They tried to break into the wizard's room at the top, but it was locked. No matter how hard they tried, they couldn't break the door down. They used axes to try and hack the door open, but they didn't even make a mark. The General didn't believe they had tried hard enough so spent hours hammering at the door himself. Eventually he gave up, exasperated and exhausted and he ordered them all to get some sleep on the floor. He planned to leave for the sea as soon as the sun came up.

Father Rhyme lay down on the cold stone floor. His back ached and he felt older than ever. It was so sore that he stopped noticing the pain in his legs. He'd find it hard going tomorrow, but from memory it was only a day or two's walk to the coast. He knew he should have tried harder to hide his destination from the General but he would have more chances to stop him between here and the islands. He could lose them at sea, or even try and run away at the port. There would be boats there. If he could just get in one and remember how to sail it, he could leave them there stranded. He closed his weary eyes and was soon fast asleep. That night he had troubled dreams of sailing through dangerous storms.

CHAPTER FOURTEEN

HOLD ON TIGHT

Sun twinkled through the window of The Prospector's mountainside home. Relly slowly awoke and began stretching. Ogi Ogi yawned and his stomach gurgled loudly. He was always hungry first thing in the morning and he'd just been dreaming about a nice frying pan full of eggs and bacon. The best thing about his dream was the fact it came true and he awoke to find Small Bear standing at the stove with a sizzling pan of hot breakfast.

'How wondrous for my tummy,' Ogi Ogi said. 'I was dreaming of bacon and eggs and then I wake up to find you making them.'

Relly laughed. 'Do you ever think about anything other than your stomach?'

'Well no,' said Ogi Ogi. 'You see, it's always empty... look.'

Ogi Ogi pulled his shirt up and showed off his gaseous body. You could see through his green swirling body to the other side of the room. When he ate, the food went in and you could see it for a few seconds before it slowly dissolved and seemed to merge into his body.

Relly chuckled. 'Well, I suppose you've got a point. Come on let's get dressed. If the Eagle isn't there, I think we need to try and find him. We're already at least half a day behind the General.'

The two friends got ready and sat down with Small Bear to eat their breakfast. The bacon was perfectly crispy and the eggs deliciously runny. Relly mopped up the yolk with the hot buttered toast and then leant back in his chair.

'Scrummy!' he declared.

'I'm glad you liked it,' Small Bear said. 'You need a good breakfast for an adventure.'

'KEEEEEYYAAAW!' came a scream from outside. 'KEEEEEYYAAAW!'

'The Eagle!' they all cried at once.

The Prospector's head suddenly appeared through the hatch. 'Ye haw! Wakey wakey, rise and shine campers. That bird brained buzzard has finally appeared. It's time to fly.'

Ogi Ogi and Relly quickly shovelled the breakfast into their hungry mouths. As soon as they finished the four friends climbed to the top of the mountain as quickly as they were able. When they finally reached the Eagle's eyrie they were out of breath and panting loudly. The Eagle's nest sat upon a wide ledge right at the very top of the mountain. Relly and Small Bear were so excited that they tumbled over each other and ended up sprawled out on the floor.

'Hello my friends,' the Eagle said.

'You're back!' Relly cried. 'There's no time to lose, we need to get to the Needle Tower in the desert. The General has taken Father Rhyme there and we need your help because it's too far to walk and...'

'Whoa, slow down,' said the Eagle. 'I can't keep up. Take your time.'

'If you didn't have your head in the clouds all day you'd be able to concentrate and keep up with the conversation,' The Prospector said.

The Eagle flicked his huge wing in The Prospector's direction and the force of the wind it created knocked him onto his bottom. Relly, Ogi Ogi and Small Bear all fell about laughing. The Prospector picked up his hat and looked like he was about to pop, then he slapped his knee and began cackling to himself.

Relly and Ogi Ogi sat down and told the Eagle everything that had happened since they'd last seen him. When they told him about the Needle Tower, the Eagle clicked his beak in surprise. Once they'd finished, they asked him again if he could take them all across the desert to try and catch-up with the General and free Father Rhyme.

'Can you take us to the Needle Tower, pleeeeeaaaassse?' Relly asked. 'Otherwise the General and his rotten guards will find the crown before us. Then he will have the crown, the sword and the mirror. Father Rhyme left us a riddle that talked about three objects that have a very magical power when they're brought together. We don't know what the General plans to do with them but it won't be anything nice that's for sure.'

The Eagle sat up and stretched out his wings. 'I've never flown across the desert. It's very hot and I thought it went on and on forever. I've always been worried that there would be nowhere to land and find water if I got tired.'

'Well, can you take us?' Ogi Ogi said.

'Me too, me too!' shouted Small Bear.

'I've only got room to carry two of you and I'm not even sure I can fit your backpacks on as well,' the Eagle replied.

'Oh no, I so wanted to go on another adventure,' Small

Bear said in a sad voice. His bottom lip started to quiver and he looked like he might burst into tears at any moment.

'Hold your horses young'un. I say, we've got work to do here. Relly and Ogi Ogi won't be able to take that huge journal of Father Rhyme's with them. It's far too heavy and valuable. If the General gets his grubby mits on it, who knows what he'd learn about these magic objects. We'd better hole up and have a look through it to find out what ye'all are gettin into. We can make you a copy of the instructions to find the crown and while you are gone, we can read the journal and look for clues.'

Small Bear was still upset, but he now had an important job to do. There was no way Relly and Ogi Ogi could possibly read the journal while they were trying to catch-up with the General. What's more he'd learn all about Father Rhyme's exploration of Imago, and who knows what secrets lay beneath its rich leather cover?

'You're right, we'll make sure we find out all there is to know about the magic objects and what the General might try and use them for,' Small Bear said.

'Thank you,' Relly said. 'That's a very important job. There are hundreds of pages with detailed notes, poems, riddles, drawings and even puzzles. One of the pages has a copy of some markings he found in a ruined temple. It looks like a code of some sort, but he never managed to work out what it meant.'

'Decipher,' said Small Bear with a pleased look on his face.

'What is?' said Ogi Ogi.

'That's what it's called when you crack a code. Father Rhyme never managed to decipher it,' Small Bear replied.

'Hang on,' Relly said, 'what about the dream stone?

What if we need to talk to Abby and Jane to ask for their help? Hadn't we better take it with us?'

The Prospector rubbed his chin thoughtfully. 'I dare say that varmint General would love to get himself a magic stone now, wouldn't he? I think it better stay safely where I hid it. Ain't no Imagino gonna find that there stone in a hurry.'

'Well come on you two,' the Eagle said. 'It's a long way across that hot desert. You'd better climb on before I change my mind.'

The Prospector gave them each a fresh flask of water and a sandwich neatly wrapped in paper. Then he slipped Relly a small bag of gems and nuggets of gold and gave him a little wink. Relly and Ogi Ogi grabbed their bags and quickly scrambled up onto the Eagle. The Eagle shuffled around uncomfortably until he was sure they were safely positioned on his back.

'Are you ready?' the Eagle asked.

'Yes,' they both replied.

'Grab a tight hold of my feathers then, because we are about to soar through the sky,' the Eagle said.

'Just don't look down,' Relly said to Ogi Ogi.

When the Eagle finished speaking, he leapt forward and launched himself off the ledge. Suddenly the ground disappeared and they were a thousand metres up in the air. As they swooped downwards and banked to the left, Relly's ears popped and his stomach felt like it had flipped upside down. He'd flown with the Eagle before, so he knew what to expect, but this was Ogi Ogi's first time. Relly looked at him and tried to give him a little grin and a thumbs up. He had turned as close to white as Relly had ever seen. He was now a sort of light cream green. If it turned Relly's stomach upside down, who knows how he was feeling? Ogi Ogi stared back with wide-eyed terror.

The Eagle shrieked loudly with joy and then beat his wings several times to carry them back up high above the clouds. They were now level with the tops of the mountains and the clouds floated below them like marshmallows on the breeze. Relly whooped with excitement whilst he looked around and enjoyed the view. Ogi Ogi wasn't enjoying the view, he was lying flat on the Eagle's back trying to pretend he was on the ground having a nice rest.

'Isn't it awesome?' Relly shouted above the noise of the wind.

'No!' Ogi Ogi yelled.

'Keeeeyyyaaaaaaawwwhhh,' screamed the Eagle with joy.

'No need to be scared,' Relly replied. 'We've levelled out now. If you sit up a little, you will be able to see the most amazing view in the whole of Imago.'

'I don't want to fall off,' Ogi Ogi replied. 'I liked it back on the ground. It didn't move so fast and it was a lot closer to me...and it just doesn't feel right. What if I get blown away?'

'You won't! We're shielded from the wind on the Eagle's back. I promise, you will be fine,' Relly said.

Ogi Ogi sat up a little. Now they'd stopped swooping about, the wind didn't feel quite so fast. He timidly looked over the side at the ground below. The desert was a wonderful mixture of yellows, oranges and reds. Behind them, The Prospector's cottage looked like a tiny dot on the mountain plains. As they flew onwards, the sand dunes started to look like golden waves in the sea of the desert. Relly grinned and pointed to the tower.

'I can't wait to see the tower,' he shouted.

'It's so far away. Do you think we will get there before it gets dark?' Ogi Ogi replied.

'It doesn't look like we're going very quickly,' Relly said, 'but we're so high up that you can't tell. We're probably going over seventy miles per hour.'

'At least a hundred,' the Eagle cried, and then he beat his wings again. As they sped forward, Ogi Ogi grabbed hold tightly while Relly whooped with joy.

The tower grew on the horizon as the day wore on. At one point a sand storm below swept across the desert and it looked like they were flying over the top of a giant mixing bowl. The sun was just starting to dip in the sky as the tower came into view. The huge tower sat upon some dark grey rocks that just poked out of the sand. It was surrounded by a beautiful oasis which was full of lush green trees, bright plants and flowers. Against the reds and yellows of the desert, it seemed to sparkle in the late evening sun.

'Hold on!' the Eagle screeched. Ogi Ogi yelped and hung on for dear life again. The Eagle began to circle around the tower as he prepared to land. Down and down they spiralled. It felt like they were going to hit the ground at high speed, but just before they landed, the Eagle spread his huge wings wide and they drifted gently to a stop. Ogi Ogi slid off the Eagle and collapsed face-down on the ground. He dragged himself over to the nearest tree and started to hug it happily.

Relly jumped off the Eagle. 'What an absolutely whizz-bang zooper dooper loop delooper fun flight,' he said.

'I'm glad you liked it, little ones,' the Eagle replied.

'The ground,' Ogi Ogi groaned. 'It's so big and still. My tummy feels so much better on the ground. I'm not moving, it's not moving. Oh, I feel sick.'

'It's not that bad,' Relly said. 'I told you not to look down.'

'I know,' Ogi Ogi replied, 'but after you told me not to look down, I kept wanting to look down all the time!'

The Eagle hopped across to the spring and started drinking deeply from the small pond. 'Ah, water,' he gasped. 'Mmmmmmmmmmm, so clear and cool and wonderfully refreshing.'

'Come on,' Relly said, 'we'd better try and find out if Father Rhyme has been here.'

'Can't we eat first?' asked Ogi Ogi. His stomach gave a loud gurgle and then he burped loudly. 'Oops!' he said, 'It must have been the landing: I didn't mean to hiccup.'

'If that's a hiccup, I'm a giraffe!' laughed Relly.

'I always thought you had a long neck,' Ogi Ogi replied.

'Well, my friends, I must be off,' the Eagle said. 'I've left my egg for quite long enough and it's time that I went and made sure it's alright.'

'Don't leave us here, stuck in the desert,' Ogi Ogi cried.

'You need to fly to the castle first and tell the Council of Imago about the tower and how the General has captured Father Rhyme. Let them know that we're trying to get to the crown first and that they need to send help,' Relly said.

'They might know something about the crown,' Ogi Ogi added.

'But I've been away too long as it is. It will be the middle of the night by the time I reach the mountains. I must warm my egg and rest first,' the Eagle said.

'But what if the future of Imago rests on your wings?' Relly said. 'Your magnificent wings can fly through the sky and raise the alarm. You will be the hero.'

The Eagle puffed himself up. He liked the idea of being a hero. 'Well, alright then,' he said. 'I will fly to the Council at once and warn them.'

Then, with one flap of his wings, he launched himself into the air. The force of the wind sent Relly and Ogi Ogi tumbling backwards. They waved as he disappeared into the sky.

CHAPTER FIFTEEN

THE WIZARD'S LAIR

R elly and Ogi Ogi walked up to the door of the tower. It was silent and the place looked deserted. Relly had to stand on tippy-toes to reach the big brass door knocker. He knocked three times.

CLONK CLONK CLONK!

After a minute or so, he tried again.

CLONK CLONK CLONK!

'Do you think there's anyone in?' asked Ogi Ogi. 'Maybe nobody lives here any more and the General has already taken Father Rhyme off to the ocean?'

'Hello!' Relly shouted. 'Anyone home!'

'Shhhhhhhhhhhhhhhhssssssssssssssssshhhhhhhhhh,' Ogi Ogi whispered. 'What are you doing? You don't want the General capturing us as well, do you?'

'Don't be silly. If that stink-pot toy soldier was here, he'd have jumped on us already,' Relly said. 'He's like a big blundering bull rampaging around a china shop.'

'CRREEEAAAK,' went the door.

'Woof! Who goes there?' came a little voice. 'Friend or foe?'

'Friend, definitely,' Relly said.

Relly and Ogi Ogi stood back as the huge door slowly opened to reveal a collection of tired-looking Imaginos.

The first to come out was a small, scruffy-looking dog who walked up to them cautiously, and gave them each a good sniffing.

'I'm Scraffles,' he panted. 'We thought you were a friend when we heard you talking about the General and calling him a rotten stinker.'

'We've come to rescue Father Rhyme,' Ogi Ogi explained. 'The General took him away in his balloon. We need to stop him getting the magic crown or who knows what he might do?'

'I'm afraid they left this morning,' said another Imagino. She was the brightest, sparkliest thing they'd ever seen. She looked just like a cheerleader's pompom. 'I'm Pom Pom,' she said. 'I met Father Rhyme many years ago when he first came to our little paradise in the desert. He spent many months here and we became dear friends. I'd have loved to have seen him again and heard about the adventures he had when he left us, but we weren't able to help him. He managed to warn us that the General and his guards were evil, so we hid. They searched the tower and then once they'd had some sleep, and it was light enough, they left.'

'Which way did they go?' Relly asked. 'We need to catch up with them. Father Rhyme is too old to be dragged halfway across Imago.'

'It will be dark soon,' Scraffles warned them, 'you won't be able to follow the path to Red Beard's Cove at night. You could end up in the middle of the desert. I can show you the way tomorrow if you like.'

'But we're getting further and further behind,' Relly said, miserably.

'I know, but we need to rest and eat!' Ogi Ogi replied, rubbing his tummy.

'Come in, come in,' invited Pom Pom. 'We can give you some food and a bed for the night.

The Imaginos of the tower welcomed them into their home. The air was cool as they stepped gratefully into the entrance hall. A large well stood in the centre of the room. Relly looked over the side. The water inside looked clear and refreshing but he couldn't see the bottom, so it must have been very deep. They were led upstairs to a large circular kitchen. Pots and pans hung down from the ceiling, a pan of stew sat bubbling on a large stove and a long table sat in the middle of the room. They all sat around the table whilst a funny looking Imagino started to fill bowls with hot, steaming stew.

'Gerbly wobbly wibble,' said the Imagino serving the stew.

'I'm sorry?' Relly said.

'Wobbly wibble gert-monkin,' said the cook.

'That's Gobbledegook,' Scraffles said. 'He speaks Gook. You get to understand what he means when you get to know him. He wants to know if you're hungry.'

'Oh yes. My tummy's rumbling like a thunderstorm,' Ogi Ogi said.

The stew was delicious. For dessert they ate a wonderful tropical fruit salad. It was made with fresh fruits from the oasis.

Once they'd eaten they met all the Imaginos that lived in the tower. As well as Pom Pom, Scraffles and Gobbledegook, there was: Ronaldolinio, a footballer; Jelly Yum Yum, whose hair and arms were made of jelly; Derek, the rabbit; and Pixel, who looked like a robot and had wheels instead of legs. They each had their own rooms in the tower and Scraffles was keen to give them a tour.

'Come on,' said Scraffles, 'let me show you around.'

Scraffles carefully lit three oil lamps and gave one to Relly and another to Ogi Ogi.

'Don't mind the mess: that rotten General and his bogey troops turned the place upside down. Loads of Imaginos used to live here but that must have been in the time of the wizard. Now there are loads of empty rooms so there's plenty of space for you to get a good night's sleep later.'

'They aren't haunted, are they?' Ogi Ogi squeaked.

'No but one of the rooms is a mystery,' Scraffles said. 'It's been locked for years and years and nobody can find the key. I'm sure Pom Pom knows something about it but she never lets anything slip. The General and his troops spent an hour or two trying to break the door down but it wouldn't budge. Jelly Yum Yum has even tried to use his jelly hands to open the lock. He pushed his fingers into the key hole and wiggled them about but it wouldn't open.'

Relly and Ogi Ogi looked at each other, beaming from ear to ear.

'The key!' Ogi Ogi cried. 'We found a key with Father Rhyme's journal in his shop. I wonder if that's what it's for.'

He showed it to Scraffles.

'Woof woof woof!' he barked excitedly, before spinning round once while he chased his tail. 'Let's try it, come on!'

They dashed up the stairs as quickly as possible. Shadows danced on the walls of the tower as they climbed. They wound round and round the tower as the steps spiralled upwards. They were all dizzy and out of breath by the time they reached the door at the very top of the tower.

Ogi Ogi took the large iron key from around his neck and carefully slid it into the lock. It clicked into place. All three friends looked at each other excitedly. He tried to turn the key but it wouldn't budge. He tried again with both hands but the key still wouldn't move. As he strained to turn the key, he scrunched his eyes up. It was then that he noticed that the two bolts that held the iron handle to the door looked like eyes. The round door knob was like a big bear's nose and the keyhole looked like a mouth in surprise.

'Hello, hello...what have we here?' said Mr Nowhere.

Scraffles nearly jumped out of his fur. He let out a yelp of surprise and chased his tail again.

'Mr Nowhere! How are you?' Relly asked.

'Here, there and everywhere,' Mr Nowhere replied.

'Where have you been? Have you seen Father Rhyme?' asked Relly.

'I can't see him. General stinky socks has taken him across the desert to Red Beard's Cove. They're either not there yet or they haven't been near anything with a face on it. So I've no way of taking a peak,' he replied.

'The key won't budge,' Ogi Ogi said. 'I don't understand it. Father Rhyme wouldn't have left us the key if it wasn't important.'

'Surely a wizard would have a magic door?' said Mr Nowhere. 'You're going to have to say the magic words to open the door.'

'But what on Imago are they?' Relly asked, 'It could be anything. We left Father Rhyme's journal with The Prospector and Small Bear, so we haven't got any clues or anything.'

'What about the writing above the door,' Ogi Ogi said.

There was some beautiful ornate writing carved into the wood at the top of the door. It read:

Intrabit in aperto dicere

'It's Latin,' Mr Nowhere said. 'I don't suppose any of you speak the ancient language of Latin?'

'Latin?' Relly said confused.

'Yes it was the language that the Romans spoke,' Mr Nowhere replied. 'Lots of words we use today are based on Latin words, though you wouldn't think it.'

"Do any of us speak Latin?" asked Ogi Ogi.

Everyone looked blankly at each other.

'It's unlikely,' explained Mr Nowhere, 'as the language died out with the Romans. Only very clever scholars know Latin these days.'

'We're done for,' Scraffles said.

'Hang on, let me go and ask one of the Council of Imago. That pixie Mithren knows a lot of languages. Her child was obsessed with elves and ancient languages. She may well know what the translation is,' Mr Nowhere replied.

Then as quickly as he appeared he was gone. The three friends looked at each other in amazement and sat down on the steps to wait. Ogi Ogi took the key out of the lock and tried to peer into the room. It was dark inside and he couldn't make out anything. He put the key back in and tried one more time but it still wouldn't budge. He was just turning around to talk to the others when...

'Boo!' shouted Mr Nowhere.

Ogi Ogi jumped so high he nearly bashed his head on the ceiling.

Relly, Scraffles and Mr Nowhere all laughed as Ogi Ogi tried to steady himself.

'You took ages!' Relly said.

'Well it took a while to get their attention. The Council of Imago was holding an emergency meeting. That eagle of yours had arrived and told them all about the tower in the desert and the General kidnapping Father Rhyme. They weren't so interested in me and my tricks,' Mr Nowhere said.

'Did she know what it meant?' Ogi Ogi asked.

'Oh yes she's a right old clever clogs,' Mr Nowhere replied. 'The translation is "To enter say open". Aperto even sounds like open.'

Ogi Ogi quickly put the key in the lock and said 'Open!' as he tried to turn it.

'Ho Ho Ho,' Mr Nowhere chuckled deeply. 'No in Latin, it's *Apertis*.'

As he said the magic word, the lock clicked and the key turned by itself in the door. The door swung slowly open and the Imaginos found themselves looking into the Wizard's lair. The shutters were closed so it was hard to see clearly, but it was definitely full of stuff. There were huge mounds of scrolls all over the place and it looked like a mad scientist's laboratory. There were all sorts of tubes, pipes and cauldrons, which might have been used to create potions. In the centre of the room sat a huge wooden desk with a large chair behind it. The chair looked worn and the material was full of holes and rips. Relly placed his oil lamp on the desk and the three friends crowded around it. Two huge maps had been spread out on the top of the desk. One of the maps showed Imago in great detail. It showed the rainforest to the West, the huge Eastern Desert and then to the North a series of islands in the ocean. Next to the islands there was a name *Dracones Dentium*. Underneath in pencil someone had written the translation Dragon's Teeth.

'Dragon's teeth! By gumball!' Ogi Ogi shouted. 'Those islands are the only thing in the ocean. They must be the three islands that Father Rhyme was talking about in his poem.'

'Must be,' Relly said. 'There's nothing else there. That must be where he's headed. We'd better make a copy before we leave. What do you think the other map shows?'

The second map showed lots of dots with names next to them. There were notes all over the map but none of them seemed to make any sense. Some of the dots had circles going through them. It looked like someone had tried to do a dot-to-dot picture but it had all gone wrong. Pencil notes had been scribbled in the corners. The writing was the same as that in Father Rhyme's journal so it must have been his. He'd drawn a ring around one group of stars and written the word 'MILKY WAY' in capitals.

'I think it's a chart of the stars,' Relly said. 'Some Imagino must have used the telescope on the roof to make a map of the sky.'

'What telescope?' asked Scraffles.

'Father Rhyme's journal talked about a rooftop observatory with a telescope that looked up towards the sky,' Ogi Ogi said.

Ogi Ogi quickly found the spiral staircase and pulled open the hatch to the roof. He scrambled up and called for them to follow. The three Imaginos gasped in excitement. A huge brass telescope sat pointing into the night sky. The lens at the end of the telescope was the width of a truck wheel. The eye piece was tiny: it was about the same size as a 10p coin. They took turns to look through it, up to the moon and the stars. The moon's surface looked like a great big, grey desert and the stars twinkled and shone brightly when the wispy clouds weren't in the way. Relly dashed back down the stairs and grabbed the map of the stars. They spent the next hour trying to find constellations.

'Imagine what it must have been like hundreds and hundreds of years ago when the Imagino wizard was up here looking at the stars,' Relly said.

'Do you think he cast his spells up here on the roof?' Scraffles asked.

'He probably used the huge cauldron in the tower room,' Ogi Ogi said. 'Do you think he used *eye of newt* and *wing of bat*?'

Scraffles looked worried and Relly laughed.

'Don't be daft,' Relly said, 'that's what they use in the stories. I bet he used plants, precious gems and magic words. Come on, let's go and look for some spell books.'

Just as they were about to dash down the stairs, Relly felt the floor move beneath him. He felt as if he was falling, he must be on the way to visit Abby. He looked at Ogi Ogi to see if he was coming, but the world of Imago began to fade as he tumbled across the worlds.

CHAPTER SIXTEEN

THE TOAD ON THE TV

It was Friday and the girls were looking forward to the weekend. The school trip to London on Wednesday had been very exciting and they couldn't wait to chat about it. Guitar lessons at lunchtime had meant they hadn't had a chance to talk about it properly but they were having a two-night sleepover at Abby's house so there would be plenty of time for discussion and planning. After they'd finished their tea, Abby's mum gave them each a bowl of vanilla and caramel ice cream and they sat down to watch TV. The Six O'Clock News was on and Abby quickly started hunting for the controller.

'Quick, turn it over!' Jane said. 'It's the pongy news! It's full of boring stories about all the bad things in the world.'

'I can't find the controller!' Abby shouted back.

'I bet it will just be the Prime Minister droning on, turn it off,' Jane replied.

'Got it!' Abby said, her finger poised over the buttons.

'Nooooo! Don't turn over!' Jane suddenly exclaimed.

'What, what is it?' Abby asked, dropping the controller in her surprise.

'The Toad!' Jane said pointing at the TV and holding her nose.

The two girls stared at the TV as the rotund, red-faced Henry Harris-Smyth MP stood frowning into the camera, his bushy eyebrows sprouting out of his forehead like freaky caterpillars. He was standing outside the British Museum talking to the reporter Jonathan Dimbleman.

'I'm joined by the Minister for Culture, Media and Sport, the Right Honourable Henry Harris-Smyth MP. Henry, can you shed any light onto the theft from the Thonis-Heracleion exhibition?' the reporter asked.

'It's not clear how and when the thief entered the museum, but they specifically targeted the exhibition. A very rare stone slab, containing hieroglyphics which describe the worship of the God Amun-Ra, has been taken,' Henry said, his face straining with mock concern.

'What is the Government doing to stop any further thefts from the museum?' the reporter asked.

'Well, I myself am personally overseeing a review of security here. I spent yesterday checking the measures that the museum has in place to ensure our national treasures and artefacts are safe. In the meantime, the exhibition will remain closed,' Henry replied in his smug, self-important voice.

The feature ended and the news moved on to the football results from the previous night. The two girls jumped up excitedly.

'What do you think he's is up to?' asked Abby.

'I don't know' Jane replied, 'but we're going to find out. Quick, get your mum's laptop and we can look up the God Amun-Ra on the internet.'

The two girls began to search the internet for stories and information on the lost city and Amun-Ra. After a few false results they eventually found a detailed report from the adventurer who originally discovered the city. He described one of the temples they'd discovered and what was written on the slabs they found.

Amun Ra was the King of Gods. He was the champion of the poor and the protector of the weak. He would appear to those who worshipped him. He travelled to them from another world where he was the King of all others. His followers believed that they could travel to other worlds if they worshipped him. The main temple in Thonis-Heracleion contained an altar with a gateway which was said to lead to them.

'Do you remember what the smelly toad said to us at the exhibition?' asked Jane.

'No,' Abby replied.

'He said "I very much look forward to visiting Imago myself one day",' Jane said.

'You're right!' Abby gasped. 'I didn't think anything of it at the time, but you don't think the slab has anything to do with Imago, do you?'

'Well, they talk about travelling to another world, and Imago is another world,' Jane said. 'What if the Egyptians had found a way to travel to other worlds like Imago? That thieving toad might try and get to Imago. I bet Relly and Ogi Ogi wouldn't like it if they found that great big smelly oaf lumbering around sticking snotty hankies in people's pockets. We need to stop him!' Jane said.

'We need to get it back,' Abby said.

'What?' Jane replied.

'The stone slab of course,' Abby said.

'But how on Earth are we going to find him and then steal it back?' asked Jane.

'Well, it's not stealing, it's recovering a stolen object,' Abby said importantly. 'My dad was talking about a meeting in the town tomorrow. They want to build a great big carpark on a field next to the town. There's going to be a planning meeting at the town hall tomorrow and I'm sure he said the snotty toad would be there. He wanted to go but he said we were too busy.'

'We should go. We might be able to get it back from him, or at least find out where he's hidden it,' Jane said. 'You'd better tell your dad that we want to go to the meeting. Who wants a great big concrete carpark on a beautiful field anyway? We had a picnic in that field last year with cake and jelly and everything.'

Abby found her dad. He was busy trying to fix a broken computer. Her dad liked to fix things but he usually had to break them first. He thought he could improve them, so he'd start taking them apart and adding to them, but then when he put them back together they never worked and there were always bits left over that didn't seem to fit anywhere.

'Dad, can we go to the planning meeting tomorrow?' Abby asked.

'The meeting at the Town Hall?' he asked, raising his eyebrows in surprise.

'Yes, we don't want them to build a car park on the field. It will spoil the wonderful view of the valley and we won't be able to have picnics there anymore,' Abby said.

'OK,' he said. 'I'm a bit surprised as I thought you and Jane wanted to go to the cinema. I want to go to the meeting myself but I didn't think we'd have time.'

'So we can go?' asked Abby.

'Yes but it might be a bit boring, you know, lots of grown-up stuff,' her dad replied.

Abby skipped back to Jane and the two girls dashed upstairs. They got themselves ready for bed and then huddled together in Abby's room to plan their investigation tomorrow. Normally they'd eat far too many sweets and stay up late. They'd only go to bed when Abby's mum came in and told them off for dancing around the room, but they wanted to make sure they were ready for anything because tomorrow they were going to take on the horrid museum thief.

The next morning they were up and dressed early. They wanted to get a good seat near the front so they could be near the stinky MP. They ate their cereal quickly before scampering through the house looking for Abby's dad. They finally found him in the office surrounded by computer parts.

'Come on, dad,' Abby implored, 'we don't want to be late.'

'So, you really want to go to the planning meeting?' he asked. 'I didn't think you were serious. It's not going to be much fun.'

'Come on dad, think of the field,' Abby replied, grabbing his arm and dragging him downstairs.

It was a short drive to the Town Hall and the girls giggled with excitement in the back of the car. Abby's dad looked in the car mirror with a confused look on his face. He was really pleased that the girls had taken an interest in the new car park but it seemed a bit odd: they normally wanted to go bowling and share an enormous ice cream.

By the time they arrived, the meeting was already getting busy. A lot of people wanted to hear about the plans for the car park and there were only a few seats left at the front. The girls rushed across the room and grabbed three seats. Henry Harris-Smyth entered and took his place at the front of the room with the rest of the planning team. Another lady stood up and outlined the Council's plans for the car park. The car park would take up a whole field and there would be new spaces for twenty coaches and sixty cars.

'Can I take any questions?' the lady asked.

A man sitting behind the girls stood up: 'The new car park is being built on an area of outstanding natural beauty. It's not right, our countryside should be protected and I think that the car park shouldn't ever be built.'

Henry Harris-Smyth stood up and stuck his large belly out. He looked like an angry baboon in a tweed suit. He glared at the man. After he'd waited for absolute silence, he spoke. 'The town's high street is dying. The shops are closing. We need a car park so more people can visit the town. I'm afraid you don't really understand business, Sir. No, you have no head for commerce. In fact you, Sir, don't know what makes the world go round.'

Once he'd finished, he smiled smugly and began to pick wax out of his ear. His big fingers looked like horrid sausages being forced into the side of his head.

Another man stood up and pointed at the MP. 'You don't understand trees, Sir. I am a tree surgeon. That means I am someone who looks after trees, keeps them well and makes sure they don't grow too big. There is an ancient oak tree in the middle of that field. The tree is protected and that means you can't build on the land. If you do you will kill it, and that, Sir, is illegal.'

The room erupted in chatter and the lady who was sitting next to Henry Harris-Smyth stood up and called for quiet. 'Order! Order!' she said. 'The tree is protected by a tree preservation order, but the car park will go around the tree and it will be perfectly safe.'

'That's not true,' the man replied. 'An oak tree of that size would need at least 30m of green space either side of it and you would need to use a natural surface for the car park. The plans just show a small hole in the concrete. It wouldn't last a year.'

Whilst they were talking, Henry Harris-Smyth reached into a large brown case and pulled out a folder stuffed full of papers. He began sorting through them until he found what he was looking for. He then glared at the man and began waving a piece of paper in the air.

'Stuff, piffle and nonsense!' Henry said. 'The report says that the tree will have enough space.'

Jane pointed at Henry and whispered to Abby, 'We need to have a look in his bag. He might have the stone slab or some clues about where he's hiding it.'

'He's such a bully,' Abby replied quietly. 'We won't be able to get near it on our own. I wish Relly and Ogi Ogi were here to help us. We need a distraction so we can search his bag while no one is looking.'

Another lady in the audience stood up. The girls nudged each other in excitement: it was their teacher Mrs Fowler. Mrs Fowler waited until the hall went quiet before speaking. 'I would like to ask our Member of Parliament a question. Under the Protection of Badgers Act 1992, it's illegal for badgers to be persecuted or their setts harmed, is it not?'

'Yes,' Henry Harris-Smyth replied. 'That is correct, but I don't see...'

'The car park will be built on top of a badger's sett, which will need to be moved before construction can begin,' Mrs Fowler replied.

He looked totally lost for words. Mrs Fowler stood staring at the great big Toad while his red face started to go redder and redder. After several minutes, he jumped up and began waving his arms in the air.

'Badgers! Badgers! Badgers are vermin,' he shouted. 'They carry diseases. They kill cattle. If they were on my farm I'd get my shot gun and I'd shoot them all. Bang! Bang! Bang! Every last one of them, the overgrown black and white rats.'

Mrs Fowler smiled slowly, 'I'm afraid, Sir, they aren't on your farm and as this is public land, they are protected.'

The room was now silent and Mrs Fowler and the stinking MP were locked in a staring competition. His face had gone deep red and he looked like a big beetroot. The girls could see the veins on Henry's neck throbbing, whilst Mrs Fowler just smiled calmly as her cool blue eyes stared back at him.

'You need to pretend you're ill,' Abby said.

'What?' Jane replied.

'Pretend you're going to be sick and head towards the desk at the front. While they're looking at you, Relly and I will try and look in his bag,' Abby said.

'But what if they catch you?' asked Jane.

'Don't worry we'll be OK,' Abby reassured her.

Jane stood up and put her hand to her mouth. 'I'm going to be sick,' she blurted out.

People jumped up to get out of her way as she pushed past them trying to get out of the row of chairs. Abby moved in the other direction and quickly made her way to the side of the hall. Jane was acting her part well. She kept moaning and jolting forward like she was going to be sick at any moment. Abby imagined Relly next to her dressed in a detective outfit. He wore a deerstalker hat like Sherlock Holmes and held a magnifying glass to help them look for clues. They ran quickly down the side of the hall and then crept behind the speakers at the front.

Jane was now in front of Henry Harris-Smyth. She'd put her hand on her tummy and had started swaying from side to side.

'Ohhhhhheeerrrr, my tummy's going to explode!' she cried. Abby's dad and Mrs Fowler had managed to get to the front and were both supporting Jane as she pretended to fall to her knees.

'Oh, I'm going to be sick!' Jane cried.

Henry Harris-Smyth quickly dragged his bag out of the way. 'Make sure you don't throw up on my shoes. They're real crocodile and you can't buy them any more.'

'Crocodile shoes,' snapped Mrs Fowler. 'Those shoes will go with your elephant ears. You, Sir, are an oaf and a baboon. I hope the badgers come along and bite you on your big red nose.'

Henry's bag was right in front of Abby. Relly put the magnifying glass to his eye and looked through it. The stone slab wasn't there. The bag contained a large bag of mint humbugs, a small hip flask, a copy of 'Shooting Times' magazine, a dirty hanky, a tatty old notebook and an egg and cress sandwich. Egg and cress, yuck! Abby thought she might be sick. She absolutely hated smelly egg sandwiches. Relly pointed at the notebook and Abby quickly grabbed it and put it under her jumper. Before anyone could notice, she dashed back around to where Jane was lying on the floor groaning. She imagined Relly standing on the desk in front of the horrible MP. Henry Harris-Smyth's breath smelled as if he hadn't brushed his teeth for years. Relly was holding his nose and pretending to faint like Jane. Abby ran around to the front of the desk.

'Come on, Jane,' Abby said. 'You just need some fresh air.'

Abby grabbed Jane's hand and pulled her up so she could whisper into her ear.

'We didn't find the slab, but Relly and I managed to get the old Toad's notebook,' she whispered. 'Come on, let's get out of here before he notices something's wrong.'

Abby helped Jane out of the hall. Abby's dad was quite worried about her. She'd come for a sleepover and now she was ill. He thought he should probably take her home.

'Shall I ring your mum?' he asked. 'If you're feeling ill I can ring the doctor.'

'That's OK, Mr Thompson,' Jane said. 'I feel fine now. It was just so hot and stuffy in there. That horrible Henry Harris-Smyth's big red face made me feel sick.'

Her dad started doing an impression of the red-faced MP and the girls giggled. Abby's dad listened to them having fun and he knew she was alright. He thought it strange that she'd had such a funny turn, but it was a crowded room and their MP was an odious man. As he drove them home, the two girls began reading through the notebook. Relly studied each page with a magnifying glass looking for clues. Towards the back they found his notes on the stone slab. In the middle of the page they found the word 'IMAGO' in capital letters.

CHAPTER SEVENTEEN

RED BEARD'S COVE

The General slowly twirled his moustache as he sat on the side of the ship deep in thought. He enjoyed playing with his moustache. He'd slowly pull at its edges until it stretched as far as possible and then he'd let it ping back into place. It was long and curled at the edges and he thought it made him look very important.

He'd commandeered the fastest ship in the cove. The crew hadn't been very willing but they'd soon got going once Lundy and the other two nit wits had given them a prod. Nothing a good clip round the ear or a boot up the bum couldn't sort out. All was going well with his plan. The old rhyming fool would soon lead him to the final piece of the puzzle. He smiled to himself as the anchor was raised and the stolen ship slowly moved out into the ocean.

Back at the Needle Tower the three Imaginos were waking up and stretching. They were extremely tired after a late night. First, Relly had returned from his adventure with Abby and he'd told them about Henry Harris-Smyth MP's notebook and the missing slab. Then they'd stayed up copying the map of Imago and after that they'd had to make up their beds for the night. A long day stretched ahead of them and they needed to leave as early as possible to catch up with the General and Father Rhyme. As soon as the red sun appeared on the horizon, Scraffles woke them up.

'Yaaaaawwwwwnnnnn,' groaned Ogi Ogi, stretching.

'I feel like I've only been asleep for ten minutes,' Relly complained.

'Woof, woof, woof!' Scraffles barked as he skipped around them in circles. 'Come on, we've got to go before the sun gets high in the sky and it gets too hot.'

'Breakfast,' Ogi Ogi said. 'We can't do anything without our breakfast.'

'I will go and ask Gobbledegook to fry us some bacon and eggs,' Scraffles said, dashing out of the tower room and heading down the stairs. Ogi Ogi's tummy gurgled loudly in reply.

'Why do you think that horrid Henry man had the word Imago written in his notebook?' Ogi Ogi asked.

'I don't know,' Relly said, 'but the girls think he stole an Egyptian slab from the British Museum. The slab must have something to do with Imago. The girls have got the notebook now because Abby and I found it in his bag. Whatever it is, it means trouble alright. He was the most disgusting oaf I've ever seen. He wanted to shoot badgers and build a carpark on a pretty field in the countryside.'

'Do you think he's got something to do with the General?' Ogi Ogi asked.

'Could do,' Relly said. 'They're both nasty, stinking, rot bags.'

'We should have a look for clues or helpful things before we go,' Ogi Ogi said.

The two friends began searching the tower room. They hunted through piles of scrolls and books, but most of them were written in Latin and other languages they didn't understand. There were piles of papers everywhere which Ogi Ogi kept tripping over. Eventually he fell into a cauldron where he was stuck upside down with his legs waggling out of the top. Scraffles and Relly nearly fell over laughing as they tried to pull him out.

'Woof woof!' barked Scraffles. 'Come on, Gobbledegook is cooking us some food. You'd better hurry up or the rest of the tower will wake up and there'll be nothing left.'

'Oh no!' said Ogi Ogi in a worried voice.

They pulled him out and dashed down floor after floor of stairs. By the time they arrived, they were all out of breath and panting. The room smelled delicious. Hot crispy bacon and buttery eggs waited on their plates. The three Imaginos sat down and started scoffing the food down noisily.

'Mmmmmmm, oooooo sooo good!' Ogi Ogi said.

'Figgler-dook not. Muntunyum foo till. Muntunyum rakenteyner doosha boog!' Gobbledegook scolded them.

'He says we should eat slower or we will get tummy ache,' Scraffles said.

'Oh sorry,' Relly said. 'It's just that the food is soooo delicious and I'm so hungry.'

'Buuuuurrrrp!' Relly belched loudy. 'Oops, very sorry. I think I ate that too fast.'

'Roooka wooka booka. Bushtidda ruppa,' Gobbledegook said, rolling his eyes.

Pom Pom came in as they were finishing off their breakfast. She'd bought three packs of supplies and a letter to give Father Rhyme when they finally caught up with him.

'Here you are, my friends,' Pom Pom said. 'Scraffles will show you the way to Red Beard's Cove. Once you are there, you will need to find a ship. Keep a look out for The Black Cat. He's supposedly the fastest ship's captain in Imago. Fancies himself as a buccaneer and wears an old pirate's hat.'

'We will make sure Father Rhyme gets your letter and I will make sure the supplies go to a good home,' Ogi Ogi said, rubbing his tummy.

'Come on!' Relly said. 'We'd better get going before it gets too hot. Thanks so much for breakfast, Gobbledegook.'

'Foor conturum nerbut,' Gobbledegook replied.

The three friends gathered their things quickly. Before leaving, Relly dropped a stone into the well and made a wish. They said their goodbyes and stepped out of the tower into the glorious sun. The heat of the morning hit them as they set off. The stone tower had been nice and cool in comparison. They left the oasis and started to walk through the desert. The sun had only just risen but they could already feel the heat of the sand through their shoes. Relly thought about Father Rhyme walking across the desert all those years ago. He must have felt like a lobster in a bubbling pot of boiling water.

After a few hours of walking, the desert began to slope downwards. Small pebbles began to appear in the sand and little patches of grass started to appear. The sun was high in the sky and Relly felt like his brain was cooking in his skull. Despite the heat, they only stopped briefly to drink water before marching on for another hour.

'My head feels like a jacket potato,' Relly moaned.

'My tongue feels like a frazzled piece of bacon,' Ogi Ogi replied.

'Not far now,' Scraffles said, skipping from paw to paw.

They staggered on in the late afternoon heat. At some point they joined an old stone path. Purple and red heathers were now dotted amongst the rocks and it was looking less and less like a desert. Relly and Ogi Ogi had stopped looking at the view. They were playing a game and trying to avoid walking on the cracks of the path, so they didn't notice when Red Beard's Cove appeared. Scraffles started barking excitedly and chasing his tail. The two friends stopped and looked down at the view in awe. There in front of them was the ramshackled sea town. Colourful boats bobbed up and down on the sea in the harbour. The buildings along the seafront were all made of wood and every single one had at least one weather vane and bell of some description. The little weather vanes were gently moving and had all turned to point in the direction of the breeze. There was a market next to the sea, with lots of bustling market stalls.

'Race you!' Relly cried, before sprinting down the path.

'Hey,' yelled Ogi Ogi.

The three friends forgot their tired legs and started running towards the town. They dashed into the market square and came skidding to a stop, crashing into each other like a line of dominoes. Scraffle's legs sprawled flat out and he started spinning around in circles barking. Relly and Ogi Ogi laughed as he nearly knocked over a fish stall. The stall's owner jumped up and down angrily.

'Hey, mind what you're doing!' the Imagino said. She looked a bit like an alien who'd dressed up as a clown. She had one eye, a great big smiley mouth and a very colourful outfit. 'You need to slow down or you'll have someone over.'

'Sorry,' Relly said, 'we're looking for our friend. He's

been captured by a mean Imagino who calls himself the General. They were heading here to try and get a ship.'

'That frothspittle came through here yesterday,' the Alien said.

'Did they get a ship?' Ogi Ogi asked.

'I'll say,' the Alien replied. 'They took old Biggetty's ship. He refused to take them but some of his crew reluctantly agreed. He promised them all sorts of riches if they'd sail north for three islands. But those islands are just legend. No one's found them or been to them for years. You mark my words, it's a fool's errand.'

'Then we're sunk,' Relly said. 'He's kidnapped our friend Father Rhyme and he's trying to find the magic crown. We must stop him or who knows what he will do.'

'There's someone who might be able to help,' said the Alien, rubbing what must have been her chin thoughtfully.

'Who?' Ogi Ogi asked.

'The Black Cat. He's the closest thing to a pirate in these waters and he's got the fastest ship that ever sailed Imago,' the Alien replied.

'Where is he?' Relly asked.

'He's probably playing cards in the *'Admiral Nelson'*,' the Alien said. 'It's the public house at the end of the docks. You can't miss it, it's got a large sign outside showing a man wearing an eye patch.'

'Thanks!' they chorused in unison.

Once again the three friends dashed off, this time heading down to the docks. They sprinted past stacks of crates which were full of fish. Boats bobbed up and down on the sea as they headed to the pub. They arrived at the *'Admiral Nelson'* and clattered through the door at full speed. Ogi Ogi tripped over a table and skidded into the bar. As they entered, all the Imaginos in the pub stopped talking and turned their heads all at the same time, to stare at them with suspicious eyes.

'Oops-a-daisy,' said Ogi Ogi, a little self-consciously.

'Erm, hello' said Relly.

No one replied. There were a few seconds of silence and suddenly the Imaginos in the pub turned back to each other and carried on talking. It was as if the three friends were invisible. Unsure what to do, they approached the bar. A tall thin Imagino with several arms was cleaning glasses and stacking shelves. He was doing both things at once. He used two arms to clean glasses and the other two were placing glasses on the shelves. He was light blue and looked like he was made out of thick spaghetti.

'Hello,' Relly said, 'we're looking for The Black Cat. Have you seen him?'

'Who's asking,' came a gruff voice from the corner of the room.

The three friends looked into the corner of the room. All they could see was a pair of bright yellow eyes shining out at them. They shuffled nervously closer and the outline of an Imagino became clearer. It was a large black cat wearing a pirate's hat. A large glass of milk and a sharp, wide-bladed, shiny cutlass sat on the table in front of him. He grinned slowly, showing off several sharp white teeth.

'Are y-y-y-o-o-o-u The B-b-black Cat?' stammered Scraffles.

'I might be,' the cat replied.

'We're trying to rescue our friend Father Rhyme,' Relly said. 'He came through here yesterday with a horrid oaf who calls himself the General. They would have had some stupid looking soldiers with them. They needed a ship to sail across the Ocean to the three islands.'

'The Dragon's Teeth,' Ogi Ogi said.

'The Dragon's Teeth?' the cat said, raising his whiskers. 'They're just a legend. They don't exist. Many have looked for them, but no one has found them.'

'They do exist,' Relly said, defiantly. 'We know they do because we have a map.'

'Oh really?' the cat replied, twirling a whisker thoughtfully. 'And where would three young scallywags like you find such a map?'

'In the Wizard's tower in the desert,' Relly said. 'Father Rhyme left us the key to open the room at the top of the tower. We found the map there and made a copy.'

'Is that so?' said the cat. 'Well, well, well, I'd like to hear a bit more of your tale. Pull up a chair and I might be able to find the cat you're looking for.'

Relly and Ogi Ogi began to tell the cat their tale. They started at the very beginning, with Grollum being arrested and locked up in the dungeons. They told him about Princess Marjorie and how she'd changed once she'd played again with her now grown-up child, Mrs Fowler. But the General had fled the castle and was trying to find three magic objects. Once he'd got them he was bound to try and take over Imago or unleash some sort of wrongness on everyone. He'd kidnapped Father Rhyme and they were heading for the islands to try and find the crown. The cat stopped them there and asked them to describe what they knew about each object. Once they'd finished, the cat gave a deep purr before he spoke.

'Well my friends,' he said. 'You've found The Black Cat, but you can call me Thomas.'

'Thomas?' Ogi Ogi said. 'Do you know Tabitha? We

took shelter in her cottage once when the guards were chasing us.'

'By my paws, Tabitha! A kinder Imagino you couldn't ask to meet,' said Thomas.

'Have you got a ship?' Relly asked.

'A ship? My friends I have THE ship! The Barracuda! My crew and I have the fastest ship in the whole of Imago. We are the most fearsome band of pirates on the Endless Ocean. If anyone can catch up with your friend, we can.'

'Really? You will help us?' Relly asked.

'Of course I will. That fish-faced General and his clumsy soldiers came charging through here yesterday. I was just coming into the docks when I saw them leaving. The whole town was in uproar. He'd stolen Biggetty's ship and half of the store's supplies. If we'd been in port, he'd have felt the edge of my sword,' Thomas said, his paw gently stroking the curved blade of the fearsome-looking cutlass.

'We must hurry. Poor Father Rhyme is far too old to be kidnapped and taken to sea. He may get sea sick,' Ogi Ogi said.

'We will need to buy a good deal of food and water for such a long sea voyage,' Thomas advised. 'I will need to talk to the crew and see how much treasure we have to spare.'

'Would this help?' asked Relly. He reached into his pocket and pulled out the small bag of gems and gold that The Prospector had given him.

'By jingo, treasure!' Thomas cried. 'That's more than enough for the journey. Why you could buy half the town with that,' He picked up the cutlass and raised it in the air dramatically. 'Come on me hearties, it's time for us to haul the anchor and chase the General down.'

The rest of the pub cheered and stood up and they were suddenly surrounded by a strange assortment of Imaginos. Thomas picked up his bag and led them out of the Admiral Nelson. They strode down to the docks and as they went, Imaginos waved to the cat and called his name. His ship was the last one in the docks. It was truly a beauty and stood twice as tall as the others. Using his cat skills Thomas sprang lightly onto the ship's deck. He quickly let down the gangway and the three friends clambered excitedly aboard.

Relly gave Thomas two gems and he sent his crew ashore to buy the supplies they needed. Imaginos scurried backwards and forwards with crates and barrels. Thomas noted their contents down in a book, making sure they had enough food and water. Once he was satisfied, he gathered the crew and told each what their role would be on the voyage. Relly was to be something called 'the starboard lookout' and Ogi Ogi was instructed to keep watch over the port.

'I need to look out for something called a "star board" but I don't know what it is,' said Relly, feeling anxious about letting the Pirate Captain down. At that moment a tall, white rabbit with long, droopy ears and wearing a pink dress, laughed and stopped by the two friends.

'I couldn't help over-hearing,' she said as she put down the enormous basket of carrots she was carrying onto the ship. 'I guess this is your first time at sea?'

'Yes it is, and we're a bit confused about what we're meant to be looking out for.'

'Starboard isn't a thing, it's a place. It means the right hand side of the ship,' she explained and turned her kind, blue eyes to Ogi Ogi, 'and I guess you're looking out port?'

'Yes I am,' replied Ogi Ogi, amazed that she knew this.

'Port means left when you're on board a ship,' she continued. 'So one of you is looking out over the right side of the ship and the other is guarding the left. You'll find ships have funny names for lots of things, and there are lots of traditions and superstitions too. Look out for the poop deck!'

Ogi Ogi wasn't sure if the white rabbit was joking but he found this hilarious and snorted with laughter.

'Come and find me if you need any more help,' laughed the rabbit and picking up her basket she continued on her way, humming a little tune to herself.

'Poop deck!' snorted Ogi Ogi.

'Oh come on, we have work to do,' said Relly, beginning to lose patience with him. And off they went to take up their positions, amazed at the various activities of the pirate crew as they prepared the ship for sailing.

Finally the mighty ship was ready to go, but just as the shout came to hoist the anchor, the two friends felt themselves falling...

CHAPTER EIGHTEEN

LOOKING FOR CLUES

The girls had spent the whole of Saturday evening reading through Henry Harris-Smyth's notebook. His handwriting was terrible. It looked like a spider had fallen into some ink and then roller-skated around the pages. Some of the pages had brown food stains on them and they even found a squashed fly. The slimy toad had drawn a smiley face next to it. The book was full of maps and Egyptian hieroglyphics, with notes about what they meant. Despite his messy writing, they could just about read the words.

'It looks like he's been searching for something,' said Jane.

'There are maps of the pyramids and notes about different Pharaohs,' Abby replied. 'There are three whole pages about the Great Pyramid of Giza in Egypt. The notes say it was built for the Pharaoh Khufu.'

'Read it out,' Jane instructed.

Using what she thought to be her best radio presenter voice, Abby began:

The great pyramids are made from giant stones. These would have needed huge diggers or cranes. None of these existed in the past and they could not have been

built by man alone. Who helped them build these great
temples?

The pyramids are aligned with the stars. It is quite
possible that the Egyptian kings used them to travel
to other worlds. Where are these other worlds? Could
one of them be the world where Douglas lives?

'Blimey!' Jane explained. 'He sounds completely bonkers!'

The last passage in the notebook had a drawing of a
stone slab. It looked strangely familiar and they were sure
that this was the one that had been taken from the British
Museum. There weren't any notes to explain what it meant
because it hadn't yet been translated into English. They
would need to find out what each of the hieroglyphics
meant before they could translate it all into English and
work out its meaning.

They asked Abby's dad if they could go to the public
library on Sunday. They didn't tell him that they wanted
to translate some ancient Egyptian writing into English
because he'd have thought that very odd. Instead they
made an excuse and said that they wanted to find out
about the local countryside to see if they could stop the car
park being built. Abby's dad said the library was shut, but
he was really pleased to see them taking such an interest in
the countryside.

They had to wait until Monday to use the school's
library at lunchtime. The morning's lessons seemed to go
by in slow motion. They had maths before lunch and it had
turned into the longest lesson ever. They were attempting a
test on their times tables and had to answer 200 questions.
The girls kept looking at the clock to see what time it was
but the hands didn't seem to be moving at all. The last five

minutes were the worst. Jane found herself watching the second hand as it tick, tick, ticked around the clock. As soon as the bell went, they scarpered off to the lunch hall and ate their packed lunches in double quick time, cramming the food into their mouths without noticing what they were eating. Abby didn't even bother to eat the tasty piece of cake that her mum had packed in her lunch box. As soon as they were able, they dashed off to the library.

The two girls were out of breath and red in the face when they arrived. Mildred Marsh and Arthur Moss were on duty. In their rush to get there, the girls had forgotten to bring their library cards. Mildred wasn't going to let them in.

'No card, no books,' Mildred said, importantly. 'They're the rules and we're here to make sure they are followed.'

'Please, Mildred. We really need to look for a book on Egypt and we couldn't go to the library in town at the weekend,' Jane said.

Mildred smiled. 'You will just have to find your cards and come back tomorrow.' She stood in the doorway with both arms folded and her nose in the air.

Arthur was very interested in Egypt and he hadn't forgotten how kind the girls had been last term when Mrs Fowler had been mean to him. Strange how she'd changed so much and was now so kind and nice. She'd even helped him with his stammer, so much so it had nearly gone.

'It's OK, Mildred,' Arthur said. 'They asked me if they could come to the library earlier and I said it would be fine.'

'I suppose I can let you off this once,' Mildred said, grumpily.

'C-come on. You can have the computer over by the reading corner, it's pretty quiet there,' Arthur said.

'Thanks, Arthur,' Jane said, 'Have you got any books on Egypt or hieroglyphics?'

'We've got a couple of books on Egypt but nothing on hieroglyphics. I looked before we went on the school trip. I wanted to be able to read things while we were there.'

'Oh no,' Abby said. 'We really wanted to translate some hieroglyphics from a stone slab. We've got a copy of one from the exhibition.'

'Oh super!' Arthur said in delight. 'We could look at the British Museum's online library from the school computer. Mrs Fowler spoke to the head librarian when we visited and told him that I was interested in Egyptology. He gave me some guest login details. We can use those to log in and look at their catalogue of books.'

'Great idea, Arthur,' Jane said. 'You're an absolute star.'

Arthur fetched his notebook. His handwriting was much neater than Henry 'The Toad' Geoffrey's. He logged them on to the British Museum's website and they searched for 'hieroglyphics'. They found dozens of books and guides. Arthur opened one titled: 'Translating Egyptian Hieroglyphics'.

'This one's got pictures for all of the hieroglyphics,' Arthur said. 'I will print you out a copy so you can take it home later as well.'

'Thanks, Arthur,' they said.

Once he'd printed it the girls began studying the stone slab. Some of the pictures were whole words while others spelled out letters. Some of the pictures looked a bit like each other so it took a while to spell them out. They were half way through when Mildred Marsh appeared and told them to hurry up.

'You've got five more minutes and then the library shuts,' Mildred said.

King will travel to world of dreams _____ _____
_____ _____ _____ _____.

'When can we translate the rest of it?' Jane asked.

'This afternoon's lesson is on our topic for the term. We're doing the Egyptians and the Romans. Why don't we say we're creating an Egyptian slab like the ones we saw at the museum? We can finish translating it in class,' Abby said.

'That's a super-dooper idea!' Jane replied.

Mr Rodgers was their teacher for the afternoon's topic lesson. He was a cheerful man who always wore a colourful tie with a jumper that didn't match. He was very kind but a bit embarrassing. He helped enthusiastically with all the fun activities at the school fête taking an active part in *splat the teacher* and *pin the tail on the headmaster*. The girls thought he looked more like a children's entertainer than a teacher. Jane often wondered if he made balloon animals or performed card tricks in the evenings and at weekends.

If Mr Rodgers saw the notebook he'd wonder where they had got it so the girls kept it hidden. They carefully made a copy of the stone slab onto a large piece of paper and then used the hieroglyphics guide to translate the rest. It took a while to finish.

King will travel to world of dreams when the magic bridge is built.

'Where do you think the *world of dreams* is?' Jane asked.

'I don't know,' Abby replied.

'Oh how marvellous!' Mr Rodgers said in his squeaky voice. He had been walking around the class looking at the children's work and he stopped by the girls' desk. 'What have we here?'

'It's an Egyptian stone slab, Sir,' Jane said, 'like the one we saw at the museum. It would have been buried with the Pharaoh, when he died.'

'It's very realistic. What superb work! I think you two should do a 'show and tell' in assembly,' Mr Rodgers said, beaming at them and rubbing his hands together.

The girls groaned. They would have to stand up in front of the whole school on Friday and talk about their picture of the slab. They'd have to explain what it meant and where they got the idea for it.

'What if someone asks us about the stolen slab?' Abby said. 'It's an exact copy of the one that's gone missing.'

'Never mind about that, we'd better find out why this slab is so important before that Toad Henry does something mean,' Jane said.

'I think it must have something to do with Imago,' Abby said. 'We spoke to Relly and Ogi Ogi in our dreams and that stinky MP mentioned Imago. What if he's trying to build a bridge so he can go there?'

'We've got to warn Relly and Ogi Ogi,' Jane said. 'Who knows what that red faced buffoon will get up to if he goes to Imago.'

'I bet he'd try and take over and start bossing them all around. Before they knew it he'd be hunting foxes and badgers and trying to build car parks all over the place,' Abby replied.

'We could send Mildred Marsh to another world; one where she needs her library card,' Jane said.

'Let's imagine Relly and Ogi Ogi dressed as Egyptian priests,' Abby said.

The girls laughed as they thought about their two imaginary friends dressed as Egyptians. Mr Rodgers continued to walk around the class talking to the other children. They imagined Relly and Ogi Ogi studying the slab they'd created and then acting out a ceremony to send Mildred to Imago. Relly had a crown that looked like a cat's head made of gold and Ogi Ogi had a big staff with a snake's head at the end. Jane imagined the eyes of the staff glowing red as they chanted the words written on the slab.

'What's this, girls?' asked Mr Rodgers smiling at them. 'You seem to be very chatty. Have you got something else to say about the Egyptian slab?'

'We were just imagining the sort of ceremony they would have had,' Abby said.

Mr Rodgers was always keen to do fun things in the classroom. He was an excitable man and he'd often do experiments or act out bits of history. He went down to the front of the class and started clearing a space.

'Come on, girls,' he chirped, with much more enthusiasm than either of the girls felt. 'Bring your picture of the stone slab down to the front. Now then class, do you remember our visit to the British Museum? Jane and Abby have made an Egyptian stone slab. We're going to act out a burial ceremony.'

Jane and Abby stood up reluctantly and made their way to the front of the class. Mr Rodgers started humming a happy tune to himself as he placed a mat and cushions on the floor.

'Who's going to be the mummy?' he said, spinning round to face the class. He was waving around a roll of toilet paper and the girls couldn't imagine where he'd found it. 'The Egyptian kings were mummified when they were buried. This meant they got covered in special herbs and wrapped in bandages so their bodies lasted longer.'

All the children tried to avoid making eye contact with him as no-one really wanted to be wrapped in toilet paper.

'Come along, children,' he chirped. 'Who wants to be the King of the Pyramids? St Joan's Primary's very own Rameses the Fifth.'

All the children looked at the floor hoping he wouldn't pick them. The girls looked at each other and then both said the same pupil's name at the same time.

'Mildred!'

'Oh splendid!' Mr Rodgers said. 'Mildred, would you come up please.'

Mildred threw them both a black look as she stomped to the front of the class. She fixed them with a menacing glare as Mr Rodgers wound the toilet roll around her until only her eyes glared at the girls through a small slit. Mr Rodgers helped her lie down. She looked like an Egyptian mummy and the girls could easily imagine Relly and Ogi Ogi dancing around the mat on the floor.

'Now then girls, please translate the stone slab for the class and repeat the words for us,' Mr Rodgers said, eagerly.

'Well the man sitting and holding a staff is the King,' Jane began.

'The two sets of legs mean travelling,' joined in Abby.

The girls continued to translate the words on the slab as Relly and Ogi Ogi pretended to take part in the ceremony. They told the class that the Egyptians might have used the slab to travel to other worlds. Mr Rodgers took a piece of paper and folded it into the shape of a crown. He put it on his head and was pretending to be a priest. He shut his eyes and started muttering the word 'Om' over and over again.

Once the girls had finished explaining the slab's meaning, they both said the magic words:

'King will travel to world of dreams when the magic bridge is built.'

Relly and Ogi Ogi both jumped up in surprise. It might have been a trick of the light but the girls felt as if their imaginary friends were actually really there and everyone else would be able to see them.

Mr Rodgers jumped up and threw his arms in the air. He looked like a terrible magician who'd performed a trick that had gone horribly wrong. He was about to start talking when the bell rang for the end of school. The class quickly gathered up their things and started to leave. Jane and Abby had to help poor Mildred up. She was wiggling around on the floor like a caterpillar.

'You won't be visiting the library at lunchtime for the rest of the year, I will make sure of that,' Mildred in a strange voice which made Abby and Jane wonder whether, unlikely though it seemed, Mildred was trying not to cry.

'Sorry, Mildred,' Jane said. 'We didn't know Mr Rodgers would start acting out a burial ceremony.'

'He's as potty as you pair of idiots,' Mildred said as she stomped off.

The girls gathered up their books and pencils and made sure they put the picture of the stone slab in their bag. As they left the classroom, Relly and Ogi Ogi, began to fall back to Imago…

CHAPTER NINETEEN

VOYAGE OF DISCOVERY

Relly and Ogi Ogi tumbled back onto the docks in Imago. The gulls were swooping through the sky above them and they could smell the salty sea air. They both shook their heads, feeling a little bit dazed.

'Crickey,' Relly said, 'you don't think that rotten toad plans to use the slab to travel to Imago?'

'Looks like it,' Ogi Ogi replied. 'He must have stolen it for a reason. Do you think he's something to do with the General?'

'He wrote about Imago in his notebook,' Relly said. 'Maybe he's the mysterious person that the General talks to through the magic mirror.'

'Ahoy, me hearties!' Thomas called. 'We're about to set the main sails. Come on board and heave ho!'

The two friends scampered onboard. The crew set to work and a huge, bright green sail with a red cross in the centre filled the mast. One of the Imaginos climbed up the rigging and sat in a huge basket at the very top of the mast. This was what they called the 'crow's nest' and an Imagino sat up there to keep watch. Once the anchor was raised, they began to move slowly away from the docks. Thomas, the Endless Ocean's most fearsome pirate, waved his hat to the Imaginos on the shore as they left the harbour.

Soon they were moving quickly across the waves and all three of the ship's sails were billowing in the wind. Relly leaned over the side of the ship and the wind rushed through his purple hair. He could feel the force of the wind pushing them along. Dolphins followed the ship, jumping above the rolling waves. He'd never been on a boat before and he felt like he was flying across the bright blue ocean.

'Ogi Ogi, come and see the Dolphins,' Relly called.

'Urgh,' Ogi Ogi replied, 'can't, might be sick!'

Ogi Ogi had seated himself in the middle of the boat. He'd turned dark green and had his hands over his mouth. 'Errrrrggghh, I feel so ill,' he said.

'Meowwwwrr! Just a bit of sea sickness, you'll get used to it. You need to get to the front of the ship and keep your eyes on the horizon,' Thomas said.

'I won't ever be able to stand up again, let alone walk,' Ogi Ogi said.

Relly spent the rest of the day looking out to sea. It was one of the most beautiful things he'd ever seen. The blue waves rising up and down reminded him of a cornfield blowing in the wind. The afternoon passed quickly and the sky began to grow dark as the sun disappeared on the horizon. He found Ogi Ogi sitting in the same position holding his tummy. He'd gone purple now and had started groaning.

'We'd better look for Thomas and find out where we sleep,' Relly said.

'Sleep!' Ogi Ogi said, 'I will never sleep while I'm going up and down on this horrible barge.'

'Barge? This ship's no barge. It's the most wonderful boat that's ever been built,' Relly replied.

'Not if you're seasick it isn't,' Ogi Ogi moaned.

Relly help Ogi Ogi down to the cabins below. The ship was a maze of little corridors and rooms. Each room was perfectly planned to make sure the space was best used. The sailors slept in neat bunks which were small but comfy. They had pillows and blankets and a small rail to make sure the Imaginos wouldn't fall out of bed in rough seas. They found Thomas in his cabin at the back of the ship. He was studying the big map of the Endless Ocean that Relly and Ogi Ogi had given him and making notes in a small blue leather book.

'Ah, there you are,' Thomas smiled. 'How's the sea sickness, my young friend? Feeling any better yet?'

'No, not at all,' Ogi Ogi replied. 'I feel absolutely dreadful. I think I might be sick again any minute.'

'What you need is some nettle tea,' Thomas said. 'Drake! Drake! Come here and fetch this young man some nettle brew.'

At the mention of nettle tea Ogi Ogi's stomach let out a huge gurgle and he quickly stuck his head into the nearest bin. 'Ooh I really couldn't drink or eat a thing,' he groaned.

'You'll feel better, trust me,' Thomas said. 'Nettle tea is the only thing to help settle a sea sick stomach. Drake's a fabulous cook. Once you've had your tea, we can have supper.'

Drake brought the tea and Ogi Ogi slowly drank it down. Once he'd had the tea, he started to feel a bit better. He even managed to eat some of the fish stew that Drake brought them. While they ate, Thomas charted their journey on the map. He was trying to work out how long it would take them to get to the islands. Depending on the winds and tides, it would be ten days at least.

'Ten days!' Ogi Ogi cried. 'I shall never be able to last

ten days on this ship. My insides will be my outsides by the time we get there.'

'How will we know which way we are going at night?' Relly asked.

'The stars, my friends,' Thomas said. 'We will follow the stars and head north into the ocean. Each day I will mark our progress on this map. The sun and stars tell me in which direction we are going and I use the speed of the ship to mark how far we've travelled.'

'We saw a chart of the stars in the Desert Tower,' Relly said.

'Fascinating,' Thomas replied. 'I would have liked to have seen that. I have my own chart, but I doubt it's a patch on the Wizard's. Now I must leave you two young adventurers, I'm wanted on deck to steer the ship. Sleep well, my friends.'

Once they'd eaten, Drake showed them to their bunk. Relly was asleep in minutes but Ogi Ogi felt like he was awake for hours.

The next week passed slowly with each day seeming the same as the last. Ogi Ogi's sea sickness got better as he became used to the ship bobbing up and down on the sea. Then, on the eighth day of the voyage, the wind started to get stronger and the sky darkened. As the storm grew in strength, the waves became larger and the ship began to rock from side to side. Relly wanted to go up to the crow's nest to watch the storm, but Thomas told him not to in case he fell overboard. Ogi Ogi's sea sickness was worse than ever. He'd turned a deep purple colour and he lay in his bunk groaning. They tried to make him nettle soup but he couldn't eat a thing.

Then suddenly the ship leaned so far starboard that

they thought they'd tip over. The ship hung there for a second before flipping back and they heard a tremendous cracking noise. Suddenly the ship was alive with voices.

'Bail! Bail! Bail! Bail out the water!' the sailors cried.

Relly jumped up and ran down to the belly of the ship where water had started to come in through a crack in the ship's hull. He helped the crew as they used buckets to scoop the water out and then pass them up a line of Imaginos. The last person threw the water over the side. As they cleared the water, Thomas worked to try and patch over the hole. He had a huge piece of wood and long nails. It took all his strength to try and hold the wood in place as the water came pouring in. Two sailors helped him as he finally hammered the nails home.

'Ha ha, me hearties, a close shave that one!' he called, grinning. 'Avast! Let's ride this storm out and make for the islands.'

Raising his sword, he dashed back up to the deck of the ship. Relly was amazed. They'd nearly been sunk yet Thomas was still laughing and leaping about. He really was a fearless pirate. Relly ran back to tell Ogi Ogi all about the leak in the ship, but as the ship rolled in the waves, Ogi Ogi felt as a sick as a parrot. They eventually managed to feed him some nettle soup, but it just made him blow off and burp loudly.

The rising of the following morning's sun brought a calmer day and the storm grew weaker. Relly and Ogi Ogi were so tired that the gentle rocking of the ship and soft murmurings of the crew soon lulled them to sleep. It had only been a couple of hours before they were awoken by the loud call from deck:

'SHIP AHOY! SHIP AHOY!'

Ogi Ogi and Relly rubbed the sleep from their eyes and ran to the deck. They looked in every direction but they couldn't see a ship. Drake pointed it out to them. Far off on the horizon was a tiny dot. They could just about make out the mast and sail but it was really small.

'How far away are they?' Relly asked.

'A good mile and a half and they've got the wind,' Drake said.

'But we'll try and run em down,' Thomas shouted. 'Set the sails, trim the lines, let's reel 'em in, reel 'em in!'

The crew dashed around the ship. It looked like chaos but they each knew exactly what they needed to do. They made sure all the sails were out and as soon as they pulled them tight, the sails filled with wind and the ship set off, racing towards the dot on the horizon. They were gaining on them all the time, the space between the two vessels gradually becoming shorter, but to Relly and Ogi Ogi, progress seemed very slow. By nightfall the other ship was a little bigger, but it was still very far away.

'They've put their lights out,' Thomas said.

'What do you mean?' Relly asked.

'They've turned the ship and blown out their lanterns so we can't follow them. If they'd kept them lit we would have been able to follow their lights. We will just have to try and make for the island as best we can. But I'm not sure that we're going the right way. That storm could have blown us off course,' Thomas said.

The crew worked through the night to try and make the ship go as fast as possible. Relly couldn't sleep for excitement, so he climbed to the top of the crow's nest. He looked out over the ocean, hoping to see a glimpse of the other ship. He thought he saw a faint glow of orange on the horizon once, but then it was gone again. Morning came and the other ship had disappeared. Thomas took the huge map and laid it out on the deck of the ship.

'I can't be sure of where we are,' Thomas said. 'That storm blew so hard, we could be miles off course.'

'We can't be too far off course,' Relly replied. 'We did see the other ship.'

'Aye that's true, you wee scamp,' he said grinning. 'Come on, look lively. Hard to port and full sail ahead.'

They sailed on with the crew looking out to sea for any sign of a ship. Relly was very tired from his night's watch. He was just nodding off to sleep when a cry woke him up with a start.

'Land ho! Land ho!' an Imagino cried.

'Where? Where?' Ogi Ogi shouted. The thought of being on land made him jump for joy.

They looked and looked but they couldn't see anything. Thomas saw the two friends searching the sea and laughed.

'The gulls,' he said. 'There are seagulls. We're too far out to sea for them to be from Red Beard's Cove so there must be land. If we follow the gulls, we will find the land.'

He steered the ship to starboard and grinned wildly, his sharp teeth gleaming in the sun. 'Not long now, my friends, not long now.'

Soon the islands came into view. They looked like little spikes to begin with, which grew gradually larger and larger.

'Remember the rhyme,' Relly said.

'What did it say?' Thomas asked.

There three islands you will find:
Pick the right one and make up your mind

With the peak to your left, head for the centre
Look for the cave that you need to enter

'That one there has the highest peak. It looks like a little mountain or a volcano. Hard to starboard and I will keep that one to our left! Right me hearties, head for the middle island,' he said.

The three islands came closer. The island to the right was edged by beautiful golden sandy beaches and palm trees. They could see small hills which seemed to be covered with colourful plants and trees and a flock of pink parrots flying between the trees. The island to the left rose out of the sea like a huge spike. There didn't seem to be a beach and there were only a few trees dotted on the shoreline. The central island had its own jagged peak, but it was much smaller than the one to the left. It had a beach running down one side, with long rocky cliff faces on the other side. As they sailed closer, they could see a huge cave in the cliff face. Above the entrance there hung huge stalactites which looked like enormous white teeth in a mouth hanging over the ocean.

Relly jumped up and down for joy: 'This is it, this is it! Don't you remember the rhyme?'

Don't be afraid of the teeth overhead
Even though they may fill you with dread
Once land is made, follow the light;
You will need to reach quite a height.

'Into the cave!' Thomas cried. 'Lower the anchor to bring her in steady and slow.'

The ship plunged into the darkness and the sailors

quickly lit lanterns and hung them over the side of the boat. The ceiling of the cave was covered in multi-coloured stalactites. Ogi Ogi thought it looked like a dragon's mouth full of fire. At the far end of the cave they could see a faint light. The ship headed towards the light and there was a scraping noise as the ship landed on the pebbly beach. Thomas left three sailors guarding the ship whilst the rest of the crew, Relly and Ogi Ogi climbed down onto the beach.

'There's a passageway!' called Drake. 'The light's coming down here. It looks like there are some old stairs.'

The Imaginos started to climb the passage. It wound upwards. In some places there were stairs and in others they clambered across rocks. Water trickled down the side of the tunnel and despite the hot sun outside, inside the cave, the air felt cool.

They'd been climbing upwards for nearly an hour before the light started to grow brighter and they knew they must be reaching an opening. Around the next corner the bright sun from the entrance blinded them.

Ogi Ogi clambered out and lay down on the ground: 'Finally the ground, I'm not at sea!'

'Come on,' Relly called. 'Don't stop there, we've nearly found it! We've just got to take ten paces forward on the track and then turn to the right.'

Relly dragged Ogi Ogi to his feet and pulled him ten paces. He turned to the right and noticed a gap in the rocks that ran alongside the track. He pushed Ogi Ogi through and then squeezed through himself. There, sitting on a chair in the middle of a clearing, was Father Rhyme. He'd been tied up and there was a handkerchief stuffed in his mouth. Relly ran over and untied him.

'We're too late,' Relly cried.

Father Rhyme just smiled at him peacefully.

'Are you alright?' Ogi Ogi asked.

'Never better to see you two, I knew you'd come through,' Father Rhyme said.

'Then we're too late,' Relly said.

'Look there! The General's ship is leaving!' Ogi Ogi cried. In the distance the two friends could see the General's ship as it started its escape from the islands.

It had been over a week since Abby and Jane had translated the stone slab from the notebook. The girls were sitting in the school library trying to finish off their presentation for Friday's assembly. Mr Rodgers had asked them to present their translation as a 'show and tell', but they couldn't stop thinking about what they should do next. They were worried about how The Toad might try and use the Egyptian slab to go to Imago. They needed to get the real stone slab from him, but how? He lived in London which was miles away and even if they got all the way there, they'd never find him: millions of people lived in London. They needed a plan to get him to come back to Thornbridge.

'We need to get the horrible Toad to come back to our school with the slab,' Jane said.

'I know! We could write him an e-mail inviting him to our school,' Abby suggested.

'But why would he come?' asked Jane. She put her head to one side and squinted as she sat deep in thought. 'I've got it, we could say that we've discovered something; something to do with the lost city and the pyramids.'

'Like what?' Abby said.

'A notebook!' Jane cried, jumping up. 'That's it, we could tell him we've found an old explorer's notebook and that it's full of stuff about the Egyptians and journeying to the stars.'

'Whose notebook?' asked Abby.

'I don't know, let's search the internet and find out who discovered the pyramids,' Jane said.

'I don't think anyone discovered the pyramids,' Abby said. 'They were there already. We need to find someone who discovered some Egyptian treasure. The greedy toad is bound to come if he thinks there's some money to be had.'

'Here we are,' Jane said. 'Howard Carter was a British archaeologist and Egyptologist who became world-famous after discovering the intact tomb of the 18th Dynasty Pharaoh, Tutankhamun.'

'Tutankhamun's tomb?' Abby said.

'A tomb was an Egyptian grave, it was where he was buried,' Jane said. 'He was known as "King Tut" and his tomb contained more treasure than any other discovered. We need to write to that ugly oaf Henry and tell him that we've found a notebook and we think it belonged to Howard Carter.'

'But we haven't got Howard Carter's notebook,' Abby said.

'No, but we've got The Toad's notebook and he's bound to want it back. We just need to write to him saying we've got a notebook. He will know it's not really Howard Carter's but that it's *his* notebook; he's bound to come to the school to have a look at it,' Jane said.

'But what will we tell Mr Rodgers?' Abby said, confused.

'We can make a pretend notebook for Howard Carter and say it's our school project,' Jane said, 'If The Toad comes to the school we can say it was a mistake.'

'A mistake?' asked Abby.

'Yes, we can say we wrote to him saying we had Howard Carter's notebook, but we meant one we'd made, not a real one. We just need to get him to come to the school and to bring the stone slab,' Jane said.

'How do we know he will bring the real stone table, the one he stole?' Abby said.

'We will ask him to bring it in the e-mail. We will say something about needing a real stone slab to help us translate something and that we think he can help,' Jane replied.

'That's the sort of stupid thing the great big oaf would do,' Abby said.

The girls unpacked their pens and paper and began to plan out their e-mail. Once they'd got an idea of what they were going to write, they'd type it out on the computer and send it.

'What do you think you two are doing?' asked Mildred Marsh in a sneery voice. She'd sneaked up behind them and was trying to look at what they'd been typing.

'We're writing an e-mail for a school project,' Abby said.

'But you haven't booked the computer out. You need to fill in a form to book out the computer first,' Mildred replied.

'But there are two computers and nobody's using them,' Jane said. 'We only want to use one of them. What's wrong with that?'

'What's wrong! I'll tell you what's wrong. There are rules in the library and people need to follow them,' Mildred said, stroppily.

Arthur overheard the noise and came over to the computers. Ever since the girls' last visit to the library, Mildred had been complaining about Abby and Jane and it had got worse since the lesson in which she'd been mummified. He picked up a form and started waving it above his head. 'Here we are, here it is,' he said.

Mildred spun round angrily, 'What do you mean here it is?'

'The form. Silly me I must have forgotten to put it in on the desk,' Arthur said.

She took a long look at all three of them. 'Just you little clever clogs remember, I've got my eye on you. Don't think you can just swan in here like you own the place. I'm the head librarian and you need to ask me for permission to do things.' Then she spun on her heels and stormed off.

The girls and Arthur laughed. They showed him the e-mail that they were planning to send.

'But why on Earth do you want that horrible MP Henry Harris-Smyth to come back here?' Arthur asked.

'We saw him steal the stone slab from the British Museum when we went there on the school trip,' Jane said. 'When he came to Thornbridge recently for the meeting about the car park, we looked in his bag to see if he had it with him. All we found was this notebook. It's got all sorts of notes in it about the Egyptians and a translation from the missing stone slab. So he must have stolen it!'

'C-c-c-c-cripes!' Arthur stuttered. 'That's awful. What an absolute rotter. No wonder you think he's a toad. What do you think he's planning to do with it?'

'We think he's planning to travel to another world, or maybe trying to get someone from that world to ours. Whatever he's doing, it's bad and we need to stop him,' Abby said.

'Well you'd better be quick then. If Mildred finds out you're e-mailing that big bully, she will report me to the Head and I'm bound to lose my job as a librarian,' Arthur said.

Jane started to type up the e-mail. She described how they had been in a charity shop looking through some old suitcases, when they came across a notebook. The notebook was full of notes about Tutankhamun and they thought it might have belonged to Howard Carter, the famous explorer. To make it seem more real, they looked on the internet and found some quotes from when the king's tomb had been found.

'What about this one?' asked Abby. 'This was written on a special cup they found:'

May your ka live, may you spend millions of years, you, who love Thebes, sitting with your face to the North Wind, your eyes beholding happiness.

'That sounds mysterious enough,' Jane said.

As soon as they'd finished, they hit "send" and the two girls ran to their next lesson as the bell went.

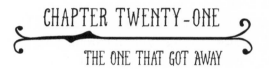

CHAPTER TWENTY-ONE

THE ONE THAT GOT AWAY

The General's ship was now a small dot on the horizon. Relly and Ogi Ogi were sitting in a heap on the floor. They felt exhausted from the climb, but worst of all a horrible feeling of failure. The General had taken the crown and was already speeding into the distance, taking full advantage of his head start. They both looked totally fed up and miserable.

'Come on,' Relly said. 'We'd better get everyone together and see if we can catch the General.'

'There's no point, he's gone,' Ogi Ogi said.

'It was all for nothing then,' Relly said, dejectedly hanging his head. 'The General's beaten us and now we will never stop him.'

'At least Father Rhyme's safe,' Ogi Ogi said, trying to think of something positive to say.

The two friends looked at Father Rhyme. He was sitting on the chair smiling to himself. As his smile grew larger, he began to chuckle to himself. The two friends looked at each other. This was very odd, they thought. Then he started to laugh out loud. Finally, he began to cry with laughter.

'Are you alright?' Relly asked. 'Have you been in the sun too long?'

Father Rhyme laughed as he said:

The General thinks he's won the hour
He has the crown, therefore the power
But the crown he took is incomplete
And can't perform a magic feat!

'It's missing a piece?' asked Relly.

Listen, I'll tell you how I did it:
I brought it here but before I hid it
I removed the crown's most precious jewel
The General, that bad, tiresome fool
Can do nothing without that stone
He'll never sit upon a throne

Father Rhyme continued describing how he'd found the mirror, the crown and the sword in the wizard's tower. He'd read dozens of scrolls describing the magic objects and the power they could yield when they were all brought together. He knew that one day an Imagino could use them to take control of Imago or worse, even try and take over the world of their children, Earth. They'd have the power to travel between worlds, and worst of all, conjure up strange monsters.

'What sort of strange monsters?' Relly asked.

The magician's scrolls weren't very clear
But it doesn't sound too good, I fear
I knew the scrolls must not be found
By one who wanted to be crowned

Father Rhyme knew he needed to hide the magical items, so he'd decided to spread them all over Imago. He took the sword to the castle and placed it with all of the others in the armoury. He took the mirror to a pyramid far to the south of Imago and then he took the crown to the islands. He sailed there using the maps the magician had created. He hid the crown and he was just about to leave the island when he had an idea. If he took the magic stone out of the crown, then it wouldn't work properly, so he went back and used a knife to prize the stone out of it.

While he'd been sailing back from the islands Father Rhyme had the strangest dreams during which he'd been able to speak to his child Fred. Fred was grown up now and had become a successful writer and poet. Father Rhyme had loved talking to him again, but he'd known he must stop. He'd started longing to use the stone to see Fred again and again. So once he'd arrived back on the mainland, he'd decided to hide the stone to make double sure that no one would ever bring all the magic objects together and use them for wickedness. He'd taken the stone and hidden it deep under the Northern Mountains, entering by a cave and following a natural tunnel until he reached a huge, open cavern. He'd left the stone there and headed quickly home to Creatown.

'It's the dream stone,' Ogi Ogi gasped. 'It's the stone we used to speak to our children. It was wonderful; we went to the top of the mountain with The Prospector and then we went to sleep and had the most amazing dreams.'

You're absolutely right, my friend
I knew you'd find it in the end
I hope you kept it tucked away
So the General cannot have his way

'We haven't got it,' Relly said.

Oh dear no, this is such a disaster
If the stone is found by a wicked master

'Oh it's OK, we've left the dream stone and your journal with The Prospector and Small Bear,' said Ogi Ogi. They've hidden them in his mountaintop home. In fact they were going to read your journal for us to try and discover more clues to help us defeat the General.'

'The General's been looking for The Prospector for months. What if his troops manage to find him?' Relly said.

To the mountains we must go
Through blistering sun, or rain or snow

Father Rhyme stood up slowly and rubbing his back, continued:

I wish I had a stick to help me down
I'm afraid I'm wobbling like a clown

He gave them a little smile and the two friends laughed at his joke. They helped him up and carefully made their way back to the others. It took them ages to get through the gap in the rocks. They got stuck at one point and Relly had to pull them both out. Once they'd squeezed through they were met by Thomas and his crew. Thomas was sitting on a big rock, using his pirate hat as a fan to keep him cool. He purred with delight when they appeared and gave Father Rhyme a huge bow.

'Ahoy matey, you've found the master of rhyme I see,' Thomas said.

'Yes, and he's all in one piece, thankfully,' Relly said. 'Can we set sail now? I'd like to make sure we catch the stinking General before he gets back to Imago and does any more damage.'

'I'd love to catch him up and scuttle him, but you two young'uns will need to rest awhile. We've got to get some supplies for the ship or we will run out of food and water in a few more days,' Thomas advised, wisely.

'Scuttle?' Relly asked.

'Sink him. I meant to sink him and send him down to the bottom of the ocean with the fishes,' Thomas said. 'But we must restock with water and food from the island before we leave.'

'There's no need to rush,' Ogi Ogi said. 'The General hasn't found The Prospector's hiding place yet. He might have the crown, but there's a piece missing, so it won't work anyway.'

'Shame, I'd love to scuttle him,' Relly said.

It took some time to climb down to the sea cave. Father Rhyme's joints ached. He wasn't as flexible as he'd been in his younger days and he'd been tied to that chair for too long. He read the letter from Pom Pom. She remembered him fondly and asked that he visit again when he could. Relly and Ogi Ogi helped him and they were soon on-board Thomas's ship.

It didn't take long to sail back to the beautiful island that they'd passed on the right. They pulled the ship up onto a beautiful golden sandy beach and the crew quickly set about finding fresh fruit and water for the journey.

Relly, Ogi Ogi and Father Rhyme sat on the beach

and watched as the crew loaded supplies onto the ship. They'd already seen bananas, coconuts and mangos being loaded on board and their mouths watered at the thought of the delicious treats which they would have to eat on the journey. Relly lay back and dug his toes into the hot sand. He was listening to the sound of the ocean and thinking what a lovely afternoon it was when he fell asleep. When he woke up, the boat was loaded and the crew was ready to go.

'There's some fine fruit and exotic parrots on this 'ere island, so I'll be coming back and that's for sure,' Thomas said. 'Come along, you land lubbers, look ship shape I'd still like to sink that dastardly General, so the sooner we get going the sooner we catch him.'

'I hope we can stop the General before he gets back to the mountains,' Relly said.

Ogi Ogi was just about to reply when they both felt that funny sinking feeling and Imago began to disappear.

CHAPTER TWENTY-TWO

YOU'RE NICKED!

Friday morning had arrived and Jane was dreading the assembly. Abby liked nothing better than to be on a stage performing to a crowd, but it wasn't Jane's idea of fun. She'd spent the whole of last night practising her slides for the presentation. It was only five minutes long and her mum had told her not to worry, but all Jane could think about was forgetting her words and everyone laughing at her. She wished Mr Rodgers had never seen their translation from the notebook. It was going to be five minutes of absolute torture and she could feel butterflies going mad in her tummy.

Her mum dropped her off at the school gate and she made her way slowly to registration. Abby gave her a little wave and patted the chair next to her. She was beaming from ear to ear. Jane sat down and their form teacher, Mr Rodgers, began to call the register.

'Moss,' said Mr Rodgers.

'Here!' Arthur replied.

Jane wasn't listening to Mr Rodgers' squeaky voice. She was wondering what she'd do if the computer stopped working in the middle of the assembly. Her mum had printed the presentation out for her, but that would be even worse because she'd have no pictures.

'Marshall...Marshall...Marshall!' said Mr Rodgers.

Jane finally heard her name and woke up from her day dream. 'Here Sir,' she said.

'Come on Jane, you really need to concentrate,' Mr Rodgers said. 'You and Abby need to be at the top of your game because we've got a special guest today.'

The girls looked at each other in shock, it couldn't be, could it?

'The Right Honourable Henry Harris-Smyth MP has heard about our Egyptian school project and has decided to visit. He's really looking forward to the assembly and he's said he'd like to meet you afterwards. What do you think of that?' Mr Rodgers asked.

Jane was speechless, as if the day couldn't get any worse! Now The Toad had turned up at the school and he was bound to try and steal back the notebook.

'Fantastic!' Abby replied happily, then, whispering to Jane, 'This is just what we wanted. The Toad has fallen into our trap.'

'Well you'd better make your way to the hall and start setting up,' Mr Rodgers said. 'The rest of the class will be over in ten minutes. I can't wait to see it.'

Abby and Jane grabbed their bags and dashed off to the hall. They needed to come up with a plan and quickly. They burst through the doors to the hall and bumped straight into Mrs Fowler.

'Hello girls,' Mrs Fowler said. 'Good to see you're here early and keen to get ready, but if you're not careful you could hurt yourselves rushing about like that.'

'It's The Toad!' said Jane.

'He's coming to get the notebook and once he's got it he will be able to get to Imago,' Abby said.

'The Toad? Whoever is that?' Mrs Fowler replied.

'Henry Harris-Smyth, the horrid MP,' said Jane. 'When we went to the British Museum he stole the stone slab from the exhibition. Don't you remember, we tried to warn you, but you thought we were being silly? Then the next day it was all over the news. We managed to get his notebook from his bag at the planning meeting and now he's come to get it back.'

Mrs Fowler thought back to the school trip. The girls *had* tried to tell her about a theft at the time, but she'd thought it was just children being daft. The museum's alarm was very loud and she thought they'd just been scared. A Member of Parliament stealing from a public museum? It didn't seem very likely.

'Ah yes, Henry Harris-Smyth the badger basher. After that planning meeting, I'm afraid he won't be getting my vote,' said Mrs Fowler.

'Look, here's his notebook if you don't believe us,' Abby said.

She handed the notebook over to Mrs Fowler who studied it carefully. The brown leather notebook had his name written inside the cover. It was packed full of notes and drawings. There were maps of pyramids, hieroglyphics, solar charts and lots of details notes. There was no way that the girls could have made this themselves, so it must have been Henry's notebook.

'Look at this bit here, this is a copy of the slab that he's stolen,' Jane said. 'There are notes here about Imago as well.'

'Imago? What's that?' Mrs Fowler asked.

'It's the world your imaginary friend lives in when you're not playing with them. It's where your friend Marjorie is now,' Jane said.

Mrs Fowler felt a little tingle of electricity run through her. She'd lived in an orphanage as a child and her only real friend, Marjorie, had been imaginary. If she'd been bored or lonely, she used to slide under her bed and enter a secret world of adventures with her Imagino. Marjorie had been a kind princess in her adventures, and the ruler of a wonderful world of imaginary friends. Jane had written a story about an imaginary friend called 'Marjorie' in Mrs Fowler's lesson last term. She thought it must have been a coincidence, but now here she was, talking about her again.

'Erm, how on Earth do you know that?' Mrs Fowler asked, uneasily.

'Look I'm really sorry, but there's no time to explain now,' Abby said. 'Can you help us hide the notebook from The Toad?'

'Yes of course,' Mrs Fowler said. 'In fact my diary looks like that notebook, so why don't we swap them.'

Mrs Fowler took her diary out of her bag. It was about the same size and colour as The Toad's. They put it on the table at the front of the hall with their notes and drawings.

'If he's really after his notebook then he's bound to try and get it back,' Mrs Fowler said. 'While he's on stage talking I will see if I can have a peak in his briefcase.'

'Miss, you're brilliant!' Jane said.

Mrs Fowler gave them a wink and went to sit at the front with the rest of the teachers. Jane and Abby sat down at the front of the hall and waited for Mr Brooke the Headmaster to arrive. A few seconds later he came into the hall, being followed by The Toad. He looked more horrid and devious than he'd ever looked before. He wore a black three-piece suit and swung gold-tipped walking cane. His horrible, over-sized feet, which Jane imagined to be covered in warts and smelling of the smelliest cheese ever, were squeezed into a pair of very expensive-looking grey crocodile skin shoes. To complete what he considered to be his most dashing look, an emerald green cravat was tied around his neck. He waddled into the room and his big belly bounced up and down. His little piggy eyes darted around, searching for the girls and when he spotted them, he shot an evil grin in their direction. Jane could see right up his nose, it looked like the end of a brush that had just been used to clean out a spider's nest.

'Morning, children,' said Mr Brooke.

'Morning, Sir,' the children replied in unison.

'We have a double Egyptian treat this morning,' Mr Brooke continued. 'Jane and Abby will be giving us a presentation on Egyptian hieroglyphics, and then we have a surprise visit from our Member of Parliament and expert on Egyptian history, Henry Harris-Smyth.'

The children all clapped politely and the girls took to the stage. Abby pictured Relly on the table next to her pointing at the slides on the screen behind her with a big stick. She started the presentation by showing the other children some different hieroglyphics and then explaining what each of the symbols meant. After this Jane nervously stood up and showed a picture of the hieroglyphics from the stone slab that Henry Harris-Smyth had stolen from the museum. The Toad was glaring at them both, his nostrils flaring like a bull's and his eyes bulging out of his head. Jane panicked and couldn't think; she'd forgotten the words she was going to say. If only Ogi Ogi were here, she'd feel safer. She imagined him dancing across the stage dressed as an Egyptian mummy. Watching him spin around on his tiptoes made her smile. She could do it, the horrid

Toad wouldn't put her off. She remembered the words and finished the presentation by reading out the translation from the stone slab.

King will travel to world of dreams when the magic bridge is built.

The Toad leapt up from his chair and started clapping in an odd, over-enthusiastic way. He looked like a great big seal slapping his flippers together. As he stomped across the stage the floor shook up and down. He stood behind the girls and stamped the end of his cane onto the floor with a loud 'crack'. Everyone jumped and then the hall was silent.

'Good morning, St Joan's Primary!' he said in a booming, oily voice. 'How utterly marvellous to see such young, eager minds studying the science of Egypt. That's right, a science I said. The Egyptians were a very clever race of people who did extraordinary things. They built huge pyramids with mighty blocks of stone and it seems they could travel across worlds. Now who can tell me the name of Egypt's wealthiest Pharaoh?'

The hall went silent as The Toad looked around beaming. 'No one? It was Amenhotep The Third. His tomb was discovered by the famous explorer Howard Carter. Have any of you heard of him? No? Well fancy you not knowing that.'

The hall was silent. The Toad turned around quickly on his heels and stared at Jane and Abby, his eyes narrowing. 'How about you two girls? Have you heard of him?' Then, before they realised what was happening, Henry Harris-Smyth MP spun around and snatched up the notebook whilst his back was turned to the hall. He stuffed it into his pocket and flashed the girls a triumphant wink. Henry thought he was having a simply marvellous time. These two meddling brats had the cheek to steal his notebook and then e-mail him about it. Well they'd messed with the wrong person because taking it back was like stealing candy from a baby, which was one of his favourite pastimes. Now he just couldn't wait to return to his large country home to prepare for his journey to Imago to take over and rule the land of imaginary friends. He'd be more important than the Queen of England. The very first thing he would do would be to find the Imaginos belonging to these two horrid, meddling brats and have them locked in irons for life.

'It was Howard Carter,' The Toad said. 'Now, I've prepared a few slides of my own which show my recent expedition to Egypt to examine the tomb of Amenhotep The Second.'

The Toad strode around the stage waving his arms as he described his trip to the school. He was very important and the Egyptian government had allowed him to visit the tomb. Every time he walked past the girls he gave them a nasty little smile. He looked like a big fat peacock showing off. Sweat was pouring off his brow and he was huffing and puffing like a cow that had got stuck in a muddy field. The girls imagined Relly and Ogi Ogi doing impressions of him as he spoke.

'Oh no, look, Mrs Fowler isn't there,' Jane whispered.

Abby looked over to the teacher's chairs. 'Where's she gone?' Abby said. 'What are we going to do now?'

'Well The Toad hasn't got the real notebook, but we still haven't got the slab back.'

'Now I hope you've enjoyed my little talk,' Henry boomed. 'I shall be heading back to London soon and I will be sure to tell let the Minister for Education know what a fine job he's doing with our schooling system.'

He finished talking and sat back down with the teachers. He took the notebook from his pocket and started looking through it. The girls watched as his face turn from smug to thunder. He went bright red and started banging his fists on his legs. Jane imagined Ogi Ogi blowing raspberries at him. Mr Brookes was about to send the pupils back to their classrooms when The Toad jumped back up.

'Hang on,' The Toad said. 'I've decided to stay and help for the rest of the day. You could clearly do with my expertise.'

Mr Brookes looked shocked. First an important politician had dropped in unannounced and demanded to come to their assembly, now he was threatening to stay all day. Things were going horribly wrong. He didn't think his day could get any worse but he looked up to see Mrs Fowler striding into the hall with two police officers. It was all too much for him and he fainted.

'Officers, arrest this man! He's stolen rare artefacts from the British Museum,' cried Mrs Fowler as she pointed at The Toad.

'Stuff, piffle and nonsense,' said The Toad. 'Do you two pavement trotters know who I am? You should be investigating real crimes. You, madame, will be put on trial for making false accusations you animal loving, badger hugger.'

'Check his bag, officers,' said Mrs Fowler.

Jane imagined Ogi Ogi dressed as police officer. He was helping the officers as they rummaged through The

Toad's bag. One of the police officers, a very tall lady, found the stone slab and held it up in the air. The other officer, a shorter man with a big beard, unsnapped a set of handcuffs and walked over to The Toad, holding them out ready. But before he could arrest him, The Toad jumped off the stage and started to run towards the hall doors. The girls were amazed, considering the size of his belly he could still get up some speed.

'Halt in the name of the law!' cried the second officer.

The Toad kept on sprinting for the door, but just before he reached it, Mrs Fowler leapt towards him. She grabbed hold of his legs and rugby tackled him to the floor. The Toad made a colossal crash as he hit the floor and the whole school building seemed to shake. Mrs Fowler jumped up, grabbed his arm and twisted it behind his back. The police officer dashed over and snapped the handcuffs onto his chubby wrists. Abby imagined Relly doing a little victory dance behind them.

'You're nicked!' said the first officer.

'You do not have to say anything. But, it may harm your defence if you do not mention when questioned something which you later rely on in court. Anything you do say may be given in evidence,' joined in the second officer.

'I've been framed!' The Toad shouted. He pointed at the girls. 'Those meddling brats took it when they went to the museum, then they lured me here and put it in my bag. I will clear my name and then I will sue you all for dragging my name through the mud.'

'I'd have thought that the mud would suit you. After all, hippos like wallowing in the mud,' said Mrs Fowler.

'You madame, you! You are the worst of the lot! You mark my words you will pay for interfering in my business,' The Toad ranted at her.

The police officers dragged him away kicking and screaming. Once he'd gone Mrs Fowler walked to the front of the hall and dismissed the school. She helped poor Mr Brooke up and sat him in a chair. Then she turned to the girls.

'I'm sorry I didn't listen to you earlier girls. Well done. If it wasn't for you Henry Harris-Smyth would never have been caught. Don't worry, I know you had nothing to do with it and I will make sure I tell the police all about the school trip,' Mrs Fowler said.

'Thanks, Miss,' Abby said. 'It's a relief to know he won't be able to get Imago. Relly, my imaginary friend, wouldn't like that at all.'

'You really must tell me more about this world of imaginary friends one day,' Mrs Fowler said. 'It sounds absolutely wonderful, I like the idea of my imaginary friend Marjorie living there.'

As the girls and Mrs Fowler left the hall, Relly and Ogi Ogi felt their children's world falling away. They felt so much happier. They might have failed to stop the General, but it didn't matter now because his grown up adult had been arrested. And of course, Ogi Ogi was looking forward to sampling the delicious fruits he'd seen being loaded onto the ship.

ACKNOWLEDGEMENTS

I 'd like to say a huge thank you to the wonderful 'Sarah from the play'. Your support, comments, edits and correct use of commas and apostrophes have helped make this book possible. Thanks also to the smaller people: Sky, Zach and Lily who make life far more fun than it would be otherwise.

Lightning Source UK Ltd.
Milton Keynes UK
UKHW041505220420
362072UK00001B/42

9 781781 329245